Smokescreen

Where would Clare watch from if she'd started the fire? Clare thought for a moment, then hurried to the back of the school, towards the playing field. She studied a distant bank of grass, which backed on to an estate of council houses.

In her dark uniform, Clare didn't expect to be seen. It was a clear night, and she could make out the silhouette of someone standing on the bank, beside a beech tree.

At the same moment, the watcher spotted Clare. He or she turned and began to ~~~~~~~ from the school. Clare ~~~~~~~~~~~~~

Other titles by David Belbin in the Point Crime series:

Avenging Angel
Break Point
Deadly Inheritance
Final Cut
Shoot the Teacher
The Beat: Missing Person
The Beat: Black and Blue

Coming soon in Point Crime:

The Alibi
Malcolm Rose

Patsy Kelly Investigates: No Through Road
Anne Cassidy

13 Murder Mysteries
Various

POINT CRIME

THE BEAT

Smokescreen

David Belbin

SCHOLASTIC

Scholastic Children's Books
Commonwealth House, 1–19 New Oxford Street,
London WC1A 1NU, UK
a division of Scholastic Ltd
London ~ New York ~ Toronto ~ Sydney ~ Auckland

First published by Scholastic Ltd, 1996

Copyright © David Belbin, 1996

ISBN 0 590 13368 3

Typeset by TW Typesetting, Midsomer Norton, Avon

Printed by Cox & Wyman Ltd, Reading, Berks.

10 9 8 7 6 5 4 3 2 1

PROLOGUE

The call came in at ten past midnight.

"Fire reported at Greencoat School."

Jan answered, "4523 responding. Any further information available?"

"Caller reports smoke rising from school site. That's all."

"Probably some kids set fire to a bin," Clare commented.

"Let's hope so," Jan said.

Clare put the flashing light on and accelerated towards the ring road.

"Greencoat's your old school, isn't it?" Jan asked.

"That's right," Clare told her. "Seems a long time ago."

But it wasn't, Jan thought, not really. Only four

and a bit years had passed since Clare left school, went to sixth form college, then on to university. Only fifteen months ago, Clare dropped out of university and joined the police force.

"It's not a bin," Jan said, as they turned off the ring road and approached the school. Massive flames licked the roof of one of the buildings, illuminating the night sky.

"Here we go," Jan muttered, as a fire engine, siren blaring, followed them into the car park. "Looks like it's starting all over again."

1

The night shift was barely two hours old. So far, Jan and Clare had visited three public houses, to make sure that they were throwing drinkers out on time; they had broken up a loud domestic argument between a husband and wife, both drunk, without an arrest; they had stopped a Fiesta with a broken tail-light and cautioned the driver; and they'd nearly run over a cyclist with no lights. When Jan asked the cyclist if he was trying to commit suicide, the youth told her where to go and what to do there. But they let him off anyway. The offence wasn't worth the paperwork which went with it.

A minute ago, Clare had felt like falling asleep. Now, as she got out of the car, her pulse raced. This was police work: hours of boredom followed by sudden fear and exhilaration. Clare had never been to a big fire before.

While Jan called the fire in to the CID Night Crime Patrol, Clare got as close to the blaze as she dared. She guided the firefighters through the maze of buildings to the centre, where the flames were. The building on fire was the main hall, which doubled as the school's theatre. At the back of the hall, Clare knew, the school used to store countless old wooden desks, which were used for exams, or as drama props.

The heat from the hall was overpowering. On stage, the vast red curtains were ablaze. Burning fabric cascaded on to the chairs where Clare used to sit in assemblies, bored out of her skull. She could see the wooden desks now, going up in flames like a funeral pyre. Clare squinted, trying to make out any signs of what started the fire, before the flames destroyed the evidence along with the school.

"Are you mad?" a firefighter yelled, pushing her aside. "Get out of here now! This area's dangerous."

Clare felt foolish. At any moment, bits of burning building could fall on her. The firefighters, unlike Clare, wore protective clothing. She ran back to the shelter of the administration block, where Jan was standing with a sour-faced man who Clare recognized as the caretaker.

"I checked it before locking up. It's not down to me."

"Could someone have hidden in there, perhaps?" Jan asked, tactfully.

"Under the stage, I suppose. I don't look there."

"You don't live on site?"

"Just down the road. I came out when I heard the sirens."

"What about the smoke alarms? Didn't they sound?"

"You can only hear them properly when you're inside the building."

"Are CID on their way?" Clare interrupted.

Jan frowned.

"Duty Officer's in Hucknall, so it'll be a while. We're to keep the scene secure."

After midnight, there was only one CID officer and an assistant on duty to cover four divisions. One detective covered Hucknall, Radford Road, Arnold and Carlton.

"I'll take a look around," Clare told Jan. "See if I can work out how they got in."

Jan nodded and started questioning the caretaker again. Clare walked round the administration building, taking the long route so that she could get safely to the other side of the hall, which connected with one of the main teaching blocks. She'd known that CID would be called in: they always were when serious arson was suspected. But she was glad that they would be a while. Clare liked the opportunity to do her own detective work.

This was the first major school fire of the year, but it wouldn't be the last. The year before, arson spread across the city's schools like an infectious disease. In one case, a couple of young men stole a car and smashed it into a classroom. Then they set the car alight, burning down half the school. In another incident, a school hall was set on fire in the lunch hour, minutes before a hundred and fifty twelve-year-olds went to register there.

The arsonists, Clare knew, were usually connected with the school. Also, they liked to watch. Clare could understand why. The fire raged in the night sky. Even at this distance, the heat was uncomfortably strong. Clare ought to be angry: this was her old school burning down. But she was also impressed. The fire had a savage, primordial power. It was hard not to stare. Was someone else watching with the same feelings – watching with pride, because they were the one who set it alight?

Where would Clare watch from if she'd started the fire? Clare thought for a moment, then hurried to the back of the school, towards the playing field. She studied a distant bank of grass, which backed on to an estate of council houses.

In her dark uniform, Clare didn't expect to be seen. It was a clear night, and she could make out the silhouette of someone standing on the bank, beside a beech tree.

At the same moment, the watcher spotted Clare.

He or she turned and began to run away from the school. Clare gave chase.

She was half-way across the field when she realized that her journey was pointless. There was a maze of streets beyond the field. She called it in, then began to run back towards the car park. If she and Jan cruised around, they might pick the arsonist up.

"Where've you been?" Jan asked. "We need to question this lot."

A gaggle of people had gathered to watch the fire. Some were young and might be students at the school. One of them could be responsible for the fire. Some wore dressing-gowns. All of them, Clare knew, would be time-wasters. They were the sort of people who slowed down to look at road accidents, thereby causing yet more accidents. The last thing she wanted to do was talk to any of them.

"I saw someone running away," Clare told Jan.

"What did they look like?"

"Just a shadow, at the end of the field. I think we should go after them."

"Did you call it in?"

"Of course I did."

"Then let someone else go after them," Jan commanded. "I'm having enough trouble keeping this lot away from the towering inferno. They've all got some kind of opinion. Maybe one of them saw something. You can start by taking all of their names and addresses."

Clare did as she was told, though she knew it was a waste of time. Odd, she found herself thinking, that the fire seemed to have been started by a single person. Usually they worked in pairs, or bigger groups. Usually, they were boys in their early to mid-teens, trying to out-dare each other.

Water gushed on to the burning building, but so far it was having little effect. While she'd been gone, a second fire engine had arrived. Firefighters were unravelling hoses. It was hard to get the audience's attention away from the show. Clare shouted at the nearest of the busybody bystanders, then began to take names.

2

Neil got the letter on Friday morning. It was there on the mat when he got in, with another from his solicitor saying that they'd be able to complete his house purchase in two weeks on Tuesday. Neil let out a double whoop and resisted the impulse to ring Clare immediately. She'd be coming off night duty too, and would have gone straight to bed. They were meeting for a drink tonight. It could wait until then. She'd be impressed, he knew she would. It was Clare's ambition to get into CID. Having a boyfriend who belonged had to be the next best thing.

Neil never set out to be a detective. It was DI Greasby who suggested he apply, back before Christmas, when Neil helped out with a surveillance job and got a result. A few weeks ago, while Clare was on her final training period at Ryton, some vacancies came up on the weekly orders. Neil went for one – without telling Clare.

He'd really thought he'd blown the interview. Neil was all right on the questions about how he'd used his detection skills over the previous year – after all, he'd helped crack that fencing operation, followed by a useful assist on a cashpoint fraud last month – but then he went dry on the equal opportunities question. He probably got over that because he had a black partner, Ben Shipman. He'd miss Ben.

Starting Monday, Neil would be on a two-week training course. When he returned, he would be allocated a tutor detective. He would work with him or her for twelve weeks. Then he'd have his first assessment as a TDC, a Trainee Detective Constable.

Neil would be sorry to leave Jan Hunt's shift, of course, but he'd been there two years. It was time to move on. And it was awkward, working on the same shift as his girlfriend. He couldn't wait to tell Clare the news.

Ruth finished work at four and went straight back to her flat, where Ben was waiting. He greeted her at the door, bleary-eyed. He looked like he'd only just got up. Which was probably the case. Ben was a police officer too, and his shift was working nights.

They hadn't seen much of each other since she got back from Ryton the weekend before.

"Ready to move?" he asked, after a kiss and a cuddle. "Or do you want a shower first?"

"What, have a shower then get all dirty again?"

Ruth changed into jeans and a sweatshirt. She and Clare were moving into a shared house. The other occupants, Sam and Steve, didn't know that both girls were in the police force. Yet. Best not to throw it in their faces the moment they moved in.

Ruth hoped to move everything in one load. Her car was only a Volkswagen Beetle, but she didn't have much stuff. This proved optimistic, though, and the ten minute drive to Forest Fields took twice as long in rush hour.

"Just leave the stuff in the hallway," Sam told them as they finished unloading the first lot. "Steve and I'll take it up for you. Yours is the middle room, right?"

"Right," said Ruth, "the smaller one."

She had let Clare talk her into that.

"Sam seems nice," Ben said, when they were back in the car. "What does she do?"

"I've no idea," Ruth said.

"Is Steve her boyfriend?"

"I don't think so," Ruth replied. "He must be ten years younger than her. He's a student, I think. He's quite a hunk, actually."

"Oh, yeah?"

Ruth gave him a cheeky smile.

"Don't worry. He's more Clare's type than mine."

"Is Neil moving Clare tonight?"

"No. Her dad is."

By six-thirty, they had everything in Ruth's room.

"Do you want me to stay?" Ben asked.

Of course Ruth wanted him to stay, but she didn't say so.

"I ought to sort the room out a bit, meet the people I'm sharing with properly."

"What about eating?"

"I'll get a take out. Maybe I could ring you later."

"Fine."

She squeezed her body against his.

"You don't mind?"

"I don't mind."

He gave her a big kiss, then left. In the corridor outside, Nick Coppola was helping his daughter to move in. Ben offered to give him a hand but Nick declined. A few minutes later, Ruth heard him leave. She went out to join Clare.

"We made it," Ruth said.

"We made it," Clare agreed.

Sam joined them on the landing. Their landlady was a tall, slender woman of thirty or thereabouts, with blonde, curly hair and an attractive, open face.

"Steve and I wanted to cook you a welcome meal," she said.

"That's really nice of you," Clare told her.

"I thought I'd give you time to get a little settled and have a wash. There's plenty of hot water for a bath or shower. We'll eat about eight-thirty. OK?"

"Great," both girls told her.

They spent the next hour sorting out their rooms. Ruth got into the shower first, then rushed to the off licence to buy a litre of wine as their contribution to the meal. Sam, it turned out, had also bought wine. The atmosphere at the table was festive. Sam served spaghetti bolognaise.

"Very appropriate food for Clare," Ruth commented.

"You're Italian?" Steve asked. He had sat himself down next to Clare.

"My father is."

"I thought I detected an accent," Sam commented. "I'd never have cooked spaghetti if I'd realized."

"This is great," Clare assured her. "I'm not that much of a cook myself."

"That's not true," Ruth insisted. "You make a mean cannelloni."

"I love cannelloni," Steve commented.

"Maybe I'll do it for you one day," Clare offered.

"Perhaps we could cook together sometimes," Steve suggested.

Ruth was hesitant.

"…er…"

"Not a rota or anything studenty," Steve corrected himself. "But it's nice to share like this."

"It is," Clare agreed, enthusiastically. "Let's do that."

"Though it might not always be easy," Ruth said, glancing at Clare as she added, "We both work shifts and we're not always home at the same time."

"Shifts?" Sam said, pushing aside the remains of her spaghetti. "Funny, I thought you said you were both students. Or do you have part-time jobs?"

"I *was* a student," Clare said, apologetically, "but I dropped out last year. I work now."

"I'll bet your job isn't as boring as mine," Sam said.

"What do you do?" Ruth asked.

"Market research. Which consists mainly of asking middle-aged women questions about their buying habits outside Marks and Spencer's."

"No," Ruth admitted, "our jobs aren't quite as boring as that."

"So what *are* you both?" Steve asked, with a jokey smile. "Why don't we play twenty questions? I know. Airline pilots. They work shifts."

"No."

"Or air stewards," Sam suggested. "You both do the same job, don't you?"

"We do," Clare said, "but not in the air. That's three questions."

"Nurses?" Steve asked. "Always handy to have a

nurse about the house."

"Not exactly," Ruth said. "But you're getting warmer."

Neil looked at his watch. Ten to ten. She'd stood him up. Or she'd forgotten, which amounted to the same thing. He'd been sitting in the Vernon, feeling like a berk, for nearly an hour. He knew that Clare was moving house today, but she'd promised to meet him for a drink. He'd hoped that Ruth and Ben might join them. He would enjoy telling his partner the good news.

But Clare hadn't come. And he didn't have her new phone number, so couldn't find out what had happened to her. Of course, he could ring her parents, get the number from them, but that would be humiliating. And how would it look, ringing Clare with a telling off on her first night in a new house? If she hadn't stood him up, he could go round with a house-warming present. As it was, he was here on his own, with no one to share his news with. Maybe he could call Ben ... but no – if Ruth was with him, it would be even more embarrassing. Or Ben might be with Charlene, the ex-girlfriend he still kept going on the side. It was too complicated. Neil ordered another pint. He would stay here until the last bus was about to go, just in case she remembered.

* * *

"I've got it," Sam said, as they drained the second bottle of wine. "You're in the police force."

"Bingo!" Ruth said, cheerily.

But neither Sam nor Steve looked like they'd won a prize.

3

For the fortieth or fiftieth time, the arsonist watched a video of the news reports after the fire.

"Police believe that the fire started just before midnight on Tuesday evening," said the lunchtime bulletin. "Our reporter, Helen Chase, spoke to the headteacher at Greencoat School, Maureen Bright."

A middle-aged woman appeared on the screen.

"Whoever did this has a very sick mind," she said. "If the Fire Brigade hadn't been called promptly, the entire school could have been burnt down. As it is, we'll be closed for a week and there'll be no assemblies or drama productions for a year. The damage will cost over a million pounds to repair. All that for a few cheap thrills."

The person watching laughed cynically. The Head was wrong. The Fire Brigade hadn't come quickly at all. The fire had been set nearly an hour before they turned up. Before that, the fire was building steadily, beautifully … a sight to behold. And, at a million pounds, these thrills were anything but cheap.

Next up on screen was a Detective Sergeant Dylan, who was in charge of the investigation for CID.

"Can you say if the fire was started deliberately?" the reporter asked.

"Home Office forensic specialists have examined the scene, but we don't know their conclusions yet. We're working on the assumption that it was arson."

"Are we seeing the beginning of another spate of school fires like the ones last year?"

The camera closed in on the sergeant's face. You could see every hair on his moustache as he replied.

"I certainly hope not. I'd like to point something out to anyone involved in last night's fire, or anyone tempted to get involved. Not only is this a very dangerous game – to yourselves and to others – but *you will be caught*. The police arrested somebody for every single one of the school fires last year. We'll do the same again. Anyone involved in arson, no matter how minor, faces serious penalties."

The picture returned to the newsroom and the viewer clicked off the set with a remote control. *You will be caught*. Who did they think they were fooling? They had nothing. No evidence. No clues. No motive. Nothing. The watcher had made one error. A police officer had seen the arsonist standing on the bank. It had been a mistake to stay there for so long. But the officer was too far away to make any kind of identification.

What this meant was that the police probably had an idea that the fire was started by one person, alone. And that was fine. The arsonist wanted the credit. They'd soon see that this was more than a schoolboy prank. Best, perhaps, to choose a name, before the press made up one of their own: something appropriate.

Phoenix. That was the first word which came to mind. A Phoenix was a mythical bird, a bird which rose from the ashes of a great fire. It was a good name for an arsonist.

Phoenix took a map of Nottingham from the shelf and considered what should be the bird's next target.

"I'm sorry," Clare said on the phone, "I completely forgot. Forgive me?"

"OK. What about tonight? An early movie and a pizza afterwards."

"Ruth and I had vague plans, but – sure, tonight. Why don't you come round, pick me up? Then you can see the house."

"Fine."

Clare put down the phone in the hall and went back up to her room. She'd prefer one of those portable phones, like they had at home. Then she could take it to her room and talk in private. But it probably wasn't practical. As she passed the bathroom, Steve came out, a white towel round his waist, his dark brown hair wet and mussy. He had a good body, she couldn't help noticing.

"Morning."

"Hi." Clare smiled bashfully, knowing it was no longer morning, wondering if he always got up at this hour. Clare was no early bird, but she was adjusting from being on lates. That was why she was still wearing her dressing-gown.

"See you later," he said, with a smile, his eyes lingering on Clare for a second longer than felt comfortable.

"Yes," she said, "later."

Clare felt guilty about Neil. Actually, she *had* remembered their date the night before, but by then it had been midnight and too late to do anything about it. She'd watched a late-night movie and gone to bed. Unable to sleep, she'd thought about Neil then, too.

Although Clare hadn't deliberately stood her boyfriend up, subconsciously she might have meant to. Her period of study was over. She was beginning a new life as a full-time police officer. They had been going out with each other, on and off, for over eighteen months, without it ever getting really serious – at least, not on her side. Soon, it would be time to make a decision about her and Neil. It couldn't be put off for much longer.

Ruth rang Ben at five past one. He'd just got up.

"What did you do last night?" she asked him.

"Watched videos. Played some music. How about you?"

Ruth told him.

"We all got talking till late. That's why I didn't phone you."

"No problem."

"How about tonight?" she asked, in her matter-of-fact, "don't mind if we do, don't mind if we don't" way.

"Sorry. I can't. It's a family thing. I'll tell you what, if the weather holds, why don't we go for a walk tomorrow, explore Sherwood Forest together?"

"Sounds nice. I'll pick you up about two."

"Great."

As Ben put the phone down, Charlene came out of the shower.

"Who was that?"

"Alice."

Charly nodded, then began to dry herself. Alice was Ben's sister, who was training to be a nurse at the Queen's Medical Centre. Ben didn't like lying to

Charly. As far as Charly was concerned, Ruth was a girl who Ben saw a bit of before Charlene moved to Nottingham. They'd sort of split up at the time. Charlene believed that his relationship with Ruth was casual, more or less platonic – which was how Ben intended it to be, at first.

This was the first time that Charly had stayed the night since moving to Nottingham. Ben had never lied, to Charly or to Ruth, before today. Until last night, when she turned up unannounced, he'd meant to finish with Charly completely, but kept putting it off. Ruth knew that Ben still saw his ex-girlfriend occasionally, but thought that they were no longer lovers.

Charly finished talcing herself and began to dress.

"What would you like me to wear for the meal tonight?"

"The purple dress," Ben said, without really thinking about it. "Dad likes you in that one."

"All right."

She kissed him on the forehead then put her coat on.

"I'll pick you up at seven. See you then."

Ruth knocked on Clare's door and went in. Already, the room was transformed: a shawl here; a vase there; a framed print of a swimming pool by David Hockney. On the wall by the bedside was a discreet crucifix.

"I wondered if you fancied going to a movie tonight," Ruth suggested. "There's a new…"

"Tonight? Sorry," Clare said. "I have to go out with Neil to make up for last night. Though if you and Ben wanted to…"

Ruth shook her head.

"Ben's got some family thing."

"You're not invited?"

"I've never even met his family. It's as if he's ashamed of me."

Clare shook her head.

"Ben's not like that. Give him time. It's only been a few weeks. And believe me, you're better off not knowing your boyfriend's parents. You don't know what a drag Sunday dinner in Wollaton is. Then there's my mum and dad. They both think that Neil's wonderful, which makes it even worse when I treat him badly. They make me feel guiltier than he does."

Ruth grinned.

"That should be less of a problem now that you're living here."

Later, alone in the house, Ruth at least had time to sort her own room out properly. By nine, she'd finished and went downstairs to make a cup of tea. Funny, she thought. She'd moved here for company, but felt more vulnerable and lonely in this big old house than she'd ever done in her cosy little flat on Wellington Square. Had it been a mistake? Clare's boyfriend would soon have his own place. What if Clare decided to move in with him?

Clare said she wasn't really that keen on Neil. She wanted to keep her options open. But any fool could see that they were good together. Clare cared more for him than she liked to admit. Also, Neil was besotted with Clare. He wouldn't let her go without a fight. What Ruth wouldn't give to be loved like that.

But she wasn't a looker, like Clare or Ben's ex, Charlene. Ruth had to get by on personality, and personality wasn't a lot of comfort when you were on your own in a strange house on a Saturday night. Ruth tried to be strong, resilient. She was trying hard not to admit to herself that she was in love with Ben. She could never say so, not unless he said it first. She didn't want to scare him off.

Ruth was about to turn on the TV when she thought she heard a noise, upstairs. Had someone come in? She went back into the hall and switched on the lights.

"Hello?"

She heard another noise, but it seemed more distant. It probably came from one of the neighbouring houses. Ruth wasn't used to living in a terraced house, where you were connected so intimately with the people around you. It would probably take her a while.

She watched the end of the evening news and a

movie, a silly action adventure thing, annoyed with herself for not having something better to do. She was about to switch over to *Match of the Day* when she heard a siren in the street. A police car pulled up outside the house.

Ruth automatically went outside to see what was going on. This house was on the edge of Ruth's patch. She recognized the two officers who got out of the car, Nasreen and Brian.

"Why are you here?" Nasreen asked Ruth, as Brian joined a man in the street, two doors down. "What are you doing in plain clothes?"

"I'm not," Ruth said. "This is where I live."

"You're kidding," Nasreen replied, incredulously. "It took me twenty-five years to be able to move out of Forest Fields – and you live here by *choice*?"

"What's going on?" Ruth asked, not caring what Nasreen thought of the area.

"Break-in, two doors down," Brian told her, casually. "Hear anything?"

"Maybe. I'm not sure."

"I'll tell you what. We'll come and talk to you when we've finished with the occupants. Put the kettle on, would you?"

"Sure."

Ruth looked at her watch as she went back into the kitchen. Quarter past eleven. Late shift on a Saturday night was the worst job going. Nights varied, but on a Saturday you could count on being run off your feet for six of the eight hours, minimum.

"You say you heard a noise at about five past nine?" Nasreen asked, a few minutes later in the living-room.

"Between five and ten past," Ruth calculated. "I stood in the hall and listened, but it went away."

"What did it sound like?"

"Someone moving things about. At first I thought it was a break-in."

"Did you look outside?" Brian wanted to know.

"No. Once I was sure it wasn't happening here, I watched some TV."

"Very public spirited of you."

Ruth found herself apologizing.

"It's a noisy area. I thought I was being silly, in the house on my own."

"Don't worry about it," Nasreen said. "I'd have done the same. It wasn't serious, anyway – a student house. They got a lot, mind – two CD players, a video, a portable TV and a load of CDs."

It'd be serious if it happened to me, Ruth thought. She wasn't sure if her insurance covered her now she'd moved. She'd have to look into that.

"How did they get in?" Ruth asked.

"Not sure," Brian told her. "They didn't make a mess. The back door was open. Occupants probably forgot to lock it. Just asking to be burgled."

Someone opened the front door noisily. A

moment later, Sam and Steve came into the room. They both looked like they'd had a few drinks.

"What's going on?" Steve asked, in a loud voice. "Police convention?"

"There was a burglary," Ruth started to explain. "Two doors down."

Then there was a message on Nasreen's radio.

"Sexual assault, Seely Road."

"Thanks for the tea," Brian said, getting up. "We're off."

"Any tea left in that pot?" Steve asked.

"It's fresh, but it could do with some more water."

While Steve went to the kitchen, Ruth decided to chance a delicate question.

"I don't want to be nosy, but ... are you and him ... you know?"

"Only when I'm really hard up," Sam grinned and Ruth wasn't sure if she was joking or not. "How about you and Clare. Are you two...?"

"God, no," Ruth said. "My boyfriend's the bloke who helped move me in. And that was Clare's boyfriend who picked her up earlier."

"The skinny guy? I guessed that he was her brother."

"It's a good thing you didn't say so," Ruth explained. "Clare's brother died in a road accident the year before last. It's a sensitive subject."

"Thanks for the warning," Sam said.

Steve came back in and switched on *Match of the*

27

Day. Ruth watched, though she didn't much like football. She wondered if Ben had come back from his parents yet, or if he'd stayed the night there. She missed him.

4

The school was a mess. None of the students were meant to be in on Monday morning, but some had turned up anyway. Last week, the Head said, was mayhem, with parents, the media and endless kids milling about the school site. Clare was back on the early shift. She wouldn't mind betting that the culprit was among the kids being shooed away by the teachers. She would like to interview all of the watchers, find out what they were doing between the hours of ten and midnight on Tuesday night.

But that wasn't Clare's job. She was here at the school's request, to act as an authority figure. The teachers were back today, but the school was closed to kids for another week. However, the teachers were having trouble keeping the kids away from the burnt-down buildings.

"I remember when teachers *were* authority figures," Jan mumbled, as they drove into school.

"Now you're really showing your age," Clare told her.

DS Dylan walked across the scorched quadrangle in front of the hall, accompanied by Mrs Bright, the Head.

"Hallo, Clare," Mrs Bright said. "How are you?"

"I'm fine," Clare told her. "I'm really sorry about … all this."

"Clare used to come to this school," the Head told the sergeant.

"Really? That could be … helpful." Dylan looked at Clare. "I don't suppose you've remembered anything else about the figure you saw on the bank?"

"A silhouette," Clare said. "That was all. I couldn't even be sure what sex it was. Quite tall, so not a young kid."

"But it could have been one of ours," Mrs Bright commented, sadly.

"I'm afraid so. Have you come up with any ideas? Someone with a recent grudge against the school?"

"That's what the sergeant's asked me, again and again. There are always people getting into trouble. But I can't think of any who'd do something like this."

"The investigation's a bit bogged down," Dylan

admitted. "There was another fire at the weekend. I'm trying to see if there's a connection. But, as for this one, if we don't find a witness, the investigation could take a long time. Trouble is, with all the kids off school for so long, memories won't be fresh by the time we get to interviewing them."

"You could start with the ones over there," Clare suggested.

"Please don't," said the Head. "You'd only encourage them to stick around."

"You could go over," Dylan told Clare, "ask a few casual questions on the pretext of throwing them out. That is, if you wouldn't mind."

"No problem," Clare said, glad to have something more substantial to do.

"Where are you going?" Jan asked as Clare marched over to the bunch of kids who remained just inside the school gates.

"Bit of detective work. I won't be long."

"You haven't got long, Miss Marple. We ought to be back on the beat in a few minutes."

Clare nodded. She admired the fact that her sergeant still did foot patrol, though both of them preferred to be in a car. The two women hadn't got on at first, but now they were partners, if not yet friends. Jan was Clare's tutor during her probation period, as well as her shift sergeant. Yet she didn't throw her weight about, which Clare appreciated.

"What are you lot doing here?" Clare asked the children by the gate.

"What business is it of yours?" the biggest of the boys asked. "It's a free country."

The boy wore jeans and a new-looking leather blouson, zipped up to almost conceal the obscene words on his red T-shirt. He was thin and spotty, but seemed to think highly of himself. Clare decided to try and charm him. She put on a flirtatious smile.

"That's not a very original line," she said. "I thought you might be hanging around because you had important information to share with the police. Would I be right? Would any of you like a word with me alone?"

The boy didn't react. The sullen reactions on the other kids' faces told Clare that she wasn't being subtle enough.

"So none of you saw anything? None of you were around here late on Tuesday night by any chance?"

"Think we'd tell you if we were?" the tall boy taunted.

"I certainly hope so," Clare said, her tone becoming sarcastic, despite her earlier intentions. "It's a citizen's duty to co-operate with the police. Don't they teach you that at this school?"

"Ah, get lost."

The boy stalked off.

"What's his name?" Clare asked the others. They were silent. "Oh, come on," she added. "I've only got to go over there and ask Mrs Bright who he is."

"He's Scott James," the smallest of three girls said. "And he's a pillock. He wouldn't have the nerve to start a fire or anything like that."

"Does it take nerve?" Clare asked, trying not to sound condescending. "I'd have thought all it took was stupidity. Can you think of anyone else who fits the bill?"

More blank faces.

"Maybe Mrs Bright did it," a grinning boy with a skinhead haircut suggested, "for the insurance."

"Ha ha," Clare told him. "Now do me a favour, you lot, clear off. We've got a job to do."

As Clare walked away, the kids moved a few metres back, to just outside the school gates.

"Anything?" Dylan asked.

Clare shook her head. "There was one boy, Scott James. He was hostile and acted like he might know something, but I think he was a time-waster."

"I'll get someone to check it out."

"OK. See you."

"Hold on."

Dylan looked around. Clare realized that he was checking to see whether Jan was within earshot.

"You were first on the scene last week, weren't you?"

"Yes. With my sergeant."

"And you used to go to this school, which could be helpful."

"What are you getting at?"

Dylan played with his moustache for a moment.

"I was thinking that, if we don't get a quick result, you might be willing to act as an aide on this one, help with questioning the students and so on."

"Eh…"

Clare's heart was leaping, but she determined to play it cool. Dylan went on.

"That's if I could persuade your sergeant to spare you, of course. Would you be interested?"

"Yes. I like detective work."

"Good. Don't mention it to anyone. I'll make a formal approach by the end of the week if we're going to need you."

"What was all that about?" Jan asked, as they resumed their foot patrol.

"He asked me to talk to some kids and one of them gave me a bit of lip."

They walked on. Clare found herself thinking about Neil. On Saturday night he'd told her about his attachment to CID. He'd thought she'd be pleased, which showed how little he really knew her. In fact, Clare was jealous. Neil started a fortnight's training course today. How would he feel if, when he got back, Clare was already acting as an aide to CID? She guessed he'd get used to it.

"What are you smiling about?" Jan asked.

"Nothing," Clare fibbed, then pointed at a parked car. "Is that tax disc out of date?"

The owner of the car was just about to drive away when Jan stopped him. Clare would hate it if this was all there was to the job: traffic offences and keeping kids out of burnt-down buildings. She'd been this way since she was a little girl. Whatever she had, she always wanted more. Clare couldn't help it. It was just the way she was.

The Greencoat fire wasn't the only arson being investigated. On Saturday afternoon, someone had walked into a city centre bank with a milk bottle full of petrol, poured the fluid all over the carpet and set light to it. Two people were burnt and another two were taken to hospital suffering from shock. There was no attempt at robbery, but the fire did over ten thousand pounds' worth of damage.

Descriptions of the arsonist varied enormously. One of the cashiers thought it was a man, but couldn't say why. A customer got the impression that it was a woman. Some said the arsonist was of medium build and height; others, thin and tall. The arsonist wore a parka-style anorak with the big hood pulled over their head. Age was described as anything from teens to mid-thirties. The only thing that everyone agreed on was that he or she was white.

Ruth read the details of the attack on her station's notice-board as she was coming off shift on Monday. Like Clare, she was on earlies that week. On her way out, she bumped into Brian and Nasreen in the corridor.

"Anything come of that burglary on my street?" she asked.

Brian shook his head.

"We turned it over to CID but I doubt they'll bother with it."

"There were days," Ruth said, "when no job was too small."

"At least we got round there," Nasreen commented. "You know, once, my family's house was burgled and the police didn't show up for two days!"

"Point taken," Ruth said. "See you later. Watch out for people in anoraks carrying milk bottles."

"What?"

"Take a look at the notice-board in the parade room."

Ruth took the bus home. She thought of going to Ben's, but he'd seemed a little distant yesterday and she didn't want to crowd him. Their relationship was too new and, she feared, too fragile. *No commitments*, she'd said from the start, because it was the only way she thought she'd hold on to him.

Turning off Gregory Boulevard, Ruth saw a young man with long hair standing outside the house which had been burgled. He was talking to a woman of sixty-something who stood in the porch of the house between his and Ruth's. The long-haired guy stopped talking and turned to Ruth just before she got to her own front door.

"You got here quickly," he said. "Is there just the one of you?"

"What do you mean?"

Then Ruth realized that she was still wearing her uniform underneath her duffle-coat.

"Sorry, I'm off duty. But I live here. Tell me what happened."

"You want to watch out," the woman with the blue-rinse perm said. "They'll do your house next. I only went out for an hour. I always visit my friend Mary on Monday afternoons."

"Did they take much?" Ruth asked, in her most sympathetic voice.

"My radio. The video my son bought me, and the remote control that goes with it. That's all I've noticed so far."

"Do you have insurance?"

The old woman shook her head pathetically.

"Costs too much. At least they left the TV set. I can still watch that."

"Probably too big," the young guy said. "They took my portable on Saturday, and the CD player I got for Christmas. Police didn't seem terribly interested. Reckoned we'd left the back door open, which is rubbish. They must have broken in some other way."

Ruth commiserated with him.

"Did anyone see anything?"

The woman shook her head. She was on the verge of tears, Ruth saw.

"I don't want to go back inside," she said, quietly.

"Why don't you come into my house? I'll make you a nice cup of tea."

"But the police…"

"I'm sure this nice young man will look out for them and tell them where to find you. Will you, er…?"

"Mark. Sure."

Ruth held out her hand.

"I'm Ruth."

He shook it. Mark was probably the same age as her, Ruth realized. Yet she had described him as a "nice young man". It must be because she was wearing the uniform.

"This is Hilda," Mark said.

"Come and sit in the kitchen, Hilda."

Steve was already there, having a late lunch. Ruth told him what was going on.

"Bummer. How did they get in? Through a window?"

"I don't know," Hilda said. "I didn't really look. The back door was open, though, and I definitely locked it. You never used to need to lock your back door round here. Not until the eighties."

The eighties seemed an awfully long time ago to Ruth.

"You think it's the same people as did next door but one?" Steve asked.

"Hard to say. The police have the details. I don't."

Two minutes later, Brian and Nasreen arrived. After a few initial queries, they decided that Nasreen would ask questions here while Brian went to look over the burgled house.

"Do you mind if I go with him?" Ruth asked Hilda. "I'm curious about how they got in."

Ruth and Brian looked around the house. It was a clean job.

"He took his time," Brian pointed out.

Rather than cutting off the leads, as most burglars did, the thief had unplugged the video recorder and carefully disconnected it from the TV.

Ruth looked in the next room. It was surprisingly neat. Normally, in a burglary, you expected to find stuff all over the place.

"They don't seem to have looked for cash, or jewellery," Ruth said. "They've just gone for the really obvious stuff."

"What I'm curious about," Brian said, "is how they got in. Back door's open, like Saturday night, but she swears she locked it, and I believe her, don't you?"

"I do."

"But there are no signs of a break-in."

"Front door's got a flimsy Yale lock," Ruth said. "It could have been done with a credit card."

"It's a possibility."

"Why don't I try – see if it works?"

"Better not," Brian said. "CID might want to take fingerprints."

"You think the nine to fivers'll bother to show up for this one, do you?"

Brian laughed. "You never know."

They went upstairs. It was part of Ruth's job, but she still found it odd, going round strangers' houses, seeing the intimate details of their life exposed. It was something a police officer had in common with a burglar. This house was the same size as the one Ruth lived in with three other people. Yet Hilda occupied it alone. The house needed work. There were damp patches and two of the three first-floor bedrooms hadn't been used for years. They smelt of mildew.

"Better check the attic," Brian said. "Though I don't suppose he bothered going up there."

"Hold it," Ruth told him. "Look."

The attic clearly hadn't been used for a while either. There was a thin layer of dust on the steps. In it could be seen the traces of a pair of training shoes, going both up and down the stairs.

"Well spotted," Brian said, holding his own shoes over the prints. "Size nine, I'd say."

Nothing appeared to have been taken from the attic room. There wasn't much to disturb. A single bed, not made up. A chest of drawers, with a large crucifix above it. Brian examined the crucifix.

"The Christ figure's made out of silver," he said. "Just needs a polish. Looks like we're dealing with a stupid burglar."

"Or a sensitive one," Ruth added.

"A sensitive burglar? Pull the other one. You mean *sensitive* like *compassionate*?"

"I guess."

Ruth was already sorry she'd spoken.

"A compassionate burglar would take one look at this place, and put stuff in, not take it out." He shook his head, then added, "Some of the things you see in this job, you wonder how people keep going."

Brian paused, suddenly conscious that he'd allowed some emotion into his voice.

"Come on," he said. "Let's go and tell the old dear that it's safe to go back into her home."

5

Charlene filed five sets of case notes, then typed up a letter to a client who was being sued for slander. No one had offered her coffee, so she went to the machine to get some. At times she felt more like a clerk than a junior partner at Jagger's. An unctuous voice interrupted her as she returned to her desk.

"How's it coming along?"

Charlene smiled and looked up at her boss, Ian. He wore a black, wide-breasted suit which had been very expensive once but was now wearing thin and needed replacing. His red tie was hopelessly unfashionable and could only be explained by its belonging to his old school. He was a dinosaur – a dignified dinosaur who could be quite dashing at times – but a dinosaur nevertheless.

"Can't complain," she told Ian Jagger. "I think I can find my way round most of the office now. It wouldn't hurt if you threw some more work at me."

"April is the cruellest month," Jagger said, "but things will pick up soon. In the meantime, though, you shouldn't be typing that."

"It's as quick to do the letter myself as it is to dictate it and give it to a secretary." Charlene couldn't stop herself over-explaining. "And I write better English when I'm at the computer than when I'm dictating."

Ian Jagger frowned.

"Then you must learn to think as you talk. It's a valuable skill and will save you time in the long run. Moreover, I don't want partners typing out their own letters. It sends out the wrong messages to both clients and secretaries."

"Very well," Charlene said.

"What are you doing on Saturday?" Jagger asked.

Charlene was even more thrown.

"Um…"

"I'm sorry it's short notice," Jagger said, in a tone which was anything but apologetic, "but a valued client is moving into a new home at the weekend and I'm having a house-warming buffet for him on Saturday evening. Quite informal, but it would give you an opportunity to meet a number of important people. And, of course, to see the other partners in a less … formal setting."

"Right, well, I'll…"

"Your … er … companion will be very welcome too."

This wasn't an invitation, Charlene realized, it was a royal command.

"I'll ask him."

"Around eight."

"Fine. Thank you."

Charlene doubted very much that she'd be able to persuade Ben to go with her. Her "companion" seemed to be under the impression that Ian Jagger was some kind of racist ringleader after he defended a bunch of skinheads earlier in the year. She and Ben had argued about it several times. Ben had been convinced by a boy working for *Searchlight* magazine, but Charlene thought her boyfriend had been conned. She had a good nose for all kinds of racism, and Jagger didn't smell of it. Ben didn't seem to appreciate that lawyers couldn't choose their clients – they chose you – and racist thugs had as much right to a defence as anyone else.

True, the firm didn't have many black clients, and this was probably one of Jagger's reasons for hiring Charlene. But what was wrong with that? Law jobs were notoriously hard to get these days, when they trained twice as many people as there were jobs for them to go to. And Jagger's was a good firm, one of the few mixing civil work with a strong criminal department.

Jagger had even helped Charlene find a flat, when Ben was too busy to help. It was a small place in the Park which would do for a few months, until Ben was ready to make a commitment. Charlene was old-fashioned, and expected him to do the proposing. She'd rather live in Mapperley Park, near Ben, but it seemed tactful to keep her distance. Anyway, the Park was a posher, even more exclusive area, and nearer to work. It must be posh, because Ian Jagger lived there too, in a big house near the tennis courts. Charlene was curious to see it.

Clare waited for CID to call for her to help with the arson investigation, but they didn't. In the meantime, there was another fire at a knitwear factory in the Lace Market. It had been broken into early on Wednesday morning. Petrol was poured over large quantities of packaging before the arsonist set the place alight. This happened at seven, half an hour before the factory opened. Nearby flats had to be evacuated in case the fire spread. The factory was gutted. Twenty-eight people were likely to lose their jobs. Clare was at work, but only heard about the fire on the evening news. It didn't happen in the area covered by her station. Therefore it had nothing to do with her.

Neil rang from Epperstone every other night. It was hard for Clare to be jealous: Neil clearly found the course exciting and wanted to share what he'd learnt with her. Clare missed Neil, and told him so. Maybe it was a case of absence making the heart grow fonder. Even so, it was hard to talk intimately in the hallway of her new house, where you could easily be overheard. Clare was looking forward to seeing him at the weekend.

"The *Rocky Horror Show*'s on at the Theatre Royal," Ruth said, when they were in the Carlton that night. "I was going to get tickets for me and Ben. Why don't you and Neil come too?"

"Why not?"

"Do you want to check it with Neil, or shall I get the tickets?"

"Get the tickets. Neil'll do what I tell him to do."

Ruth laughed.

"What about you?" she said to Sam. "Fancy coming?"

Sam shook her head.

"Been there. Done that. The film and the stage show. And, no, I won't tell you how many years ago."

A long-haired guy came over and started talking to Sam. They were supposed to be having a girls' night out, but it was amazing how many people Sam knew in the busy pub. Clare and Ruth were getting to meet lots of new faces. Some of them, Clare thought, would run a mile if they knew what she and Ruth did for a living.

At a quarter to ten, Steve came into the pub, alone. He waved at the three women.

"Anyone need a drink?"

His eyes met Clare's, making it clear that it was her he was interested in.

"No thanks," she said. "Got to be going soon. Early start tomorrow."

"Mind if I join you?" he asked, as the barmaid pulled his pint.

"Yes, we do mind," Sam said, half-seriously. "Clear off. We're having a good time without you."

Steve came and sat down anyway. The conversation died.

"I meant to ask you on Friday," Clare said to Steve, "but I forgot. What course are you doing?"

"Want to play twenty questions?" Steve asked, with a mischievous glint in his eye. "What course do you think I do? Chemistry? Philosophy? Agricultural engineering?"

"You look like a scientist to me," Ruth told him.

"Languages," Clare suggested.

"Eighteen to go."

"This is boring," Sam interrupted. "Tell them, Steve."

Steve shrugged. He was wearing a leather American airman's jacket with wide wool lapels. It was probably too warm but it looked very sexy, Clare thought. He was one of those rare men who knew what to wear and how to wear it.

"I'm *not* a student," Steve told them. "Not any more. I graduated last term – in Art History, actually – and now I'm a government artist. I draw the dole."

Clare laughed dutifully though she'd heard the joke a hundred times before.

"What kind of work are you looking for?"

Steve grinned.

"I'm not. I figured that, after seventeen years of education, working for harder and harder exams, I deserve a rest. Don't you agree?"

"I guess," Clare said, dubiously.

Sam looked bored.

"While we're all here," their landlady said, "could we discuss what we're going to do about these burglaries? It looks like they're working their way down the street."

"Why don't we ask the experts?" Steve suggested.

He doesn't like me because of my job, Clare told herself. *Who cares? He's too fond of himself for his own good anyway.*

"We're not sure what kind of burglar he is," Clare said. "It could be a teenage opportunist, who sees an open door and can't resist. Or it could be a couple of professionals, with a car. Until we get a witness, it's hard to know."

"So whichever it is," Steve suggested, "he must be smart, since you've got no clues?"

"I doubt it," Clare told him. "All burglars are thick. They have to be stupid and desperate to do what they do. This one's just lucky, that's all."

"So what do we do?" Sam asked.

"I can recommend a good burglar alarm company, if that's what you mean," Ruth told Sam.

"How much do they cost?"

"Cheapest decent system would run you about five hundred."

Sam shook her head. "There's no way I could afford that, even if you three chipped in."

Clare was glad Sam hadn't asked. Neither she nor Ruth had a hundred and twenty-five quid to throw around. Steve certainly wouldn't have, either.

"The front and back doors both have decent locks," Clare said. "It might be worth putting a second mortise on the back to make it harder for a burglar to kick it in. The front door's too public for anyone to risk it."

"Is that it?" Steve asked. "Is that all they taught you?"

"There are obvious precautions," Clare continued. "It's important to put the window locks on when going out, especially now the weather's getting warmer. Don't leave doors unlocked. If we're all out of an evening, it's as well to leave a light burning, some music playing."

Ruth put a hand to her mouth and yawned.

"This is like being at work. Time for me to be going."

"I'll come too," Clare said, standing.

They bid Sam and Steve good night.

"I *thought* he didn't seem to do much work," Clare told Ruth, as they walked back along Berridge Road East.

"I wonder why he's stayed around," Ruth said. "Something to do with Sam, perhaps."

"You've got a bee in your bonnet about them being a couple," Clare complained.

"She as good as told me…"

"She was winding you up."

Clare went straight up to bed but couldn't sleep. It was Thursday tomorrow. Would DS Dylan from CID call? She listened carefully as Steve and Sam came in. Only one set of footsteps went up to the attic room. Clare was sure that Ruth was wrong. Steve was free. He hadn't once mentioned a girlfriend. But Clare wasn't free. She told herself off for being tempted by him. Even if she wasn't with Neil, it would be far too messy, going out with someone who lived in the same house as you. Although students did that sort of thing all the time. Clare still thought of herself more as a student than as a twenty-year-old policewoman. She wondered how Steve thought of her.

Phoenix bought a copy of the *Post* in the lunch hour, the early edition, and sat down in the the John Farr Rest Gardens, a small park by Clarendon College, to read it. The fire in the Lace Market had made the front page, better than the one at Greencoat had done. "*FACTORY FIRE – 30 JOBS LOST*" was the headline, with "*City burns as commuters arrive for work*" underneath. The policeman quoted was the same one who'd been on the telly after the school fire.

"'Signs are that this was arson,' DS Dylan said. 'The timing of the fire was very unusual and we're anxious to hear from people who were in the city early this morning.' Police were not at this stage linking the fire with any others in recent weeks."

Phoenix cursed. The note left at the scene couldn't have been found. The fire went even better than Phoenix expected. The note must have got burnt. But links needed to be made – a signature left behind so that responsibility could be put in the proper place. Yet, how? Anything left behind was liable to be burnt. Staying on the scene after starting the fire – to write a message on a wall, for instance – was too risky. The Greencoat fire proved that. Phoenix had stayed to watch, then had to duck in and out of alleyways to avoid being caught by a police car.

A photograph, perhaps, taken with one of those instant cameras the moment of the fire being started, posted to the press the same day – with a sketch of a Phoenix on the other side. Neat. But too neat. Unless the photo was hand delivered – too risky – there would be a day's delay before it reached the media. And there'd be the hassle of carrying the camera around. It would quickly become as incriminating as the milk bottles filled with petrol which Phoenix carried in an old-fashioned, box-style briefcase.

But a letter … that might be an idea. You'd have to be careful, with fingerprints, typeface and stuff like that. Using letters cut out of newspapers was one way, but it took ages. Better to use a typewriter – Phoenix knew where there was one which the police would never think to check – that was how to do it. Then it would be simple. Put the letter in the post, first class, the day before the job. By the time the letter arrived, the fire would be over. The responsibility would never be in doubt.

Once the letter was posted, Phoenix would be committed to starting the fire, no matter what unforeseen problems arose. But that was OK. It raised the stakes a bit higher, made the game more interesting. The only question was: *Where next?*

6

Ben was beginning to dread weekends. He wished he was working. At least, then, he wouldn't have to juggle the demands of having two girlfriends, both of whom assumed that they had first call on his time.

Out for a walk with Ruth last Sunday, she had casually mentioned going to the theatre and, feeling guilty about not being with her the night before, he'd agreed. Ben didn't know what he was thinking of. He never went to *the theatre*. And some tacky seventies revival at that. But he meant to go anyway, out of duty. That was, until Charlene rang last night and said that there was this do on Saturday night, and she couldn't go alone. It was a really big deal.

"It's to do with work, right?"

"An important client's visiting."

"You don't need me there for that," Ben said, curtly. "You know how I feel about Jagger. Sooner or later you'll find out that I'm right."

But then Charlene turned the tables on him.

"If you're so sure he's a crook, then you have to come to his buffet."

"Why?"

"Because you'll get to see him in his natural habitat, making deals, dispensing words of wisdom. We'll see if your image of him stands up next to the real person. After all, you've never actually met Ian, have you?"

Ben had to admit that no, he hadn't. Nor had he any reason to suppose that the lawyer had any idea who he was.

"So you'll come then?"

"I guess…"

He couldn't tell her that he was letting down Ruth. Charly thought that he was going out for a drink with Neil and some other friends on the force, who would understand that his girlfriend's needs came first.

"Thanks," Charlene said, affectionately. "Love you. See you tomorrow night. Bye."

But Charlene wouldn't be seeing him tonight. He'd left a message on her machine, cancelling. If he was going to stand Ruth up tomorrow, the least he could do was spend tonight with her. Ben hoped that she was free. Clare would know. He waited for Clare at the end of the shift. She was in the sergeant's office with Jan Hunt. Ben couldn't help hearing the sergeant's raised voice.

"I don't believe it! You've only been back for two weeks. I'm already one officer down because of Neil. I thought you'd be happy that he was gone. You're always complaining that working together puts too much stress on your relationship. But no. Now you want to follow him into CID."

Clare's voice in reply was firm but placatory.

"I didn't *ask* for this, you know. They asked me because I used to go to the school. You can say 'no'. Inspector Grace said it was up to…"

"Sure it is. Then I'll have you moping around about what you've missed until this arson case is cleared up. No. Go. Go. But you owe me one, Clare."

"I owe you one," Clare said, as Jan pushed the door open and swore.

"I'm late again. Dawn'll kill me."

She saw Ben.

"Looks like your partner problems are over for the time being, sunbeam. You're with me next week – at least until Neil's replaced and Clare finishes acting as an aide to CID."

"Fine," Ben said, tactfully. "I'll look forward to it."

Jan swept out of the parade room, leaving Clare alone with Ben.

"Seeing Neil tonight?" he asked her.

She nodded.

"Give him my best."

"I will. But you'll be seeing him tomorrow. We're going to…"

Ben shook his head.

"Something's come up. I need to see Ruth. Do you know if she's doing anything tonight?"

Clare frowned.

"Not as far as I know. Want to come back with me? We could share a taxi. I hate going on the bus in my uniform."

Ruth's car was outside the house when their taxi pulled up. Ben went up to her room. He wished he'd gone home to change now. The uniform was a constant reminder of the job, even when it was hanging from the wardrobe door after Ruth undressed him.

"You told me you couldn't see me today," she said, later on.

"Change of plan. I'll pay for my ticket tomorrow but…"

He explained about the buffet, as diplomatically as he could. Ruth knew that Ben still saw Charlene occasionally – he was, after all, her only friend in Nottingham. She didn't know that he'd never really split up with her. Also, Ruth had met Jagger, and knew what he was like. When Ben finished explaining, Ruth's eyes blazed.

"You're kidding! You're standing me up for *Jagger*?"

"It's not like that. It's an opportunity to find out more about him."

Ruth was having none of it. Her voice became sarcastic.

"I see. You're not going to please Charlene's boss by being the token black male at his party, you're going to *investigate* him – as if he's likely to have evidence of corruption and racism all over the house."

"Eh…" It sounded pretty weak, Ben realized.

"Get out," Ruth said. "Go on. Get out!"

She was out of bed and dressing. Ben followed suit.

"I didn't mean to…"

"I know. You didn't mean to do anything. Go with me. Keep seeing Charlene. Have your cake and eat it. Well, I'm sorry. I thought I could stand it, but I can't. You're going to have to choose, Ben."

"Don't…"

She was crying now. He wanted to hold her, but she wouldn't let him near.

"Do me one favour," Ruth added, her voice cracking.

"Anything."

Ruth's voice wavered, but the tone was hard, bitter.

"When you've made up your mind, tell me. Don't

make me work it out for myself, the way I've had to work out that you're sleeping with Charlene again."

Ben couldn't think of anything to say.

"Please leave now."

He left.

Phoenix decided that the safest thing to do was post the letter on a Saturday. That gave the Post Office two days to get it to the local media. There were no deliveries on Sunday, so, as long as the fire was set by dawn on Monday, the letter wouldn't put its sender in any danger.

But, before that, Phoenix had to sort out a signature: something eye catching to appear in the papers. The simplest, most effective thing to use would be a rubber stamp. It had to be a ready made one. Phoenix didn't have the skills needed to carve the rubber, and paying someone else to do it was risky – it would make identification too likely.

Phoenix went round the city stationery shops on Saturday morning, when they were at their busiest. Most had only a few stamps, for office use, with words like "Paid" and "Copy" in large letters. But, in Tableworks, a new shop in King John's Arcade, Phoenix found a selection of woodblocks with more creative designs on them. They were right by the counter, but below it, and the assistant had her back to them, too. The one which Phoenix found might not be the mythical bird, but it was close enough. It was child's play to slip it into a pocket. Better to be done for shoplifting than arson, after all. Phoenix walked out of the shop without buying anything.

Later, Phoenix typed out the letter. It was a long time since Phoenix had used a typewriter and an even longer time since this one had been used. Its ribbon was getting faint, but, after a bit of messing about, was still legible. Phoenix left the precise target ambiguous, just to be on the safe side, and made the note short. It was simpler to type it three times than to photocopy it, which might invite danger. Phoenix made a couple of mistakes and kept going over the end of the paper, but typed over the errors with Xs, rather than use tippex and risk leaving a finger print. Then Phoenix added the stamp at the bottom, typing in an explanation of the name, just in case. It still didn't look right, so Phoenix put the letter back into the electric typewriter and added "PS". Now, apart from one spelling mistake and some missing punctuation, it looked fine.

```
DEAR MEDIA,
            BY THE TIME YOU READ THIS,
I'LL HAVE ADDED TO MY SERIES OF
BONFIRES. HOW DID YOU LIKE THE SMELL
OF BURNING BOOKS?!
```

I DON'T WANT ANYBODY ELSE GETTING THE ~~CREI~~
CREDIT FORM WHAT IVE DONE. SO, FROM NOW
ON YOU'LL KNOW ITS ME WHEN YOU SEE MY ~~SING~~
SINGATURE BELOW

PS   YOU CAN CALL ME "PHOENIX"
      BYE FOR NOW.

When it was done, Phoenix went back into town, to the main Post Office on Huntingdon Street, where the last collection didn't go until 5p.m. on a Saturday. Wearing gloves, Phoenix put the letters, in plain brown envelopes, into the red box. There was one for the *Evening Post*, one for Radio Trent, and one for Radio Nottingham. Now all Phoenix had to do was start another fire.

7

Charlene looked ravishing. It was an unusually mild spring and she wore a white, low-cut linen dress with heels and her hair done up. The dress was too much for the assembly of middle-aged men, many of whom found it hard to keep their eyes off her. The wives gave Charlene dirty looks, as if she were trying to steal their husbands. But Ben knew that the dress was meant for him. Charly might not know about Ruth, or her ultimatum, but she'd known him long enough to be able to sense what was on his mind. Maybe she sensed that he hadn't made it up yet.

So far, Ben hadn't set eyes on the solicitor, Jagger. He'd been buttonholed by one of the firm's junior partners, who told Ben what a good impression

Charlene had made in her first month at the firm. As Charly talked to a county councillor, Ben fended off questions about his own career.

"Are you in the law, too?"

"You could say that. Charly and I met on the LLB course in London."

"*Charly?* I didn't know people called you that."

Ben looked round to see that she was by his side again.

"They don't," Charly said. "It's an old family nickname. Ben's the only one who still uses it."

"Ah."

This wasn't true, but Ben let it pass. He could see that a female solicitor wouldn't want to be known to her colleagues as Charly. Particularly not if her co-workers were all middle-class toffs like this one.

"Ah, here's our host."

Ben's first impression of Ian Jagger was his size. He was a big man. Not fat, or even overweight, but big. He wore a navy blue suit and a white shirt with frills down the front. His shoes, Ben saw at a glance, were hand-made. His face was large and almost fleshy, but his jaw was strong. Despite his size and age – nearer fifty than forty, Ben guessed – he had no double chin. Ben couldn't tell if the lawyer's black hair was dyed. He had short side-burns which turned grey at the edges to match his bushy eyebrows, making him look even more distinguished. Jagger strode through the room like power incarnate, shaking hands and kissing cheeks.

"Our guest will be here in a few minutes," Ben heard him announce, more than once. As Jagger advanced towards them, across a spacious hall and into the plush living-room, Ben wished that he could hide behind the velvet curtains. Charlene smiled graciously and the pantomime villain kissed her on both cheeks.

"And this is Ben."

"A pleasure to meet you."

Ben was surprised to see that Jagger was actually an inch or two smaller than he was. His handshake was dry and firm. Ben could think of nothing to say to him.

"I gather we've you to thank for Charlene wanting to work in Nottingham."

"Yes."

"We're very lucky to have her."

"So am I," Ben felt obliged to say.

Jagger should have moved on by now, but he still stood in front of Ben, gripping his hand. Ben had stared at his photograph in the local paper, learned to hate his image. Yet, in the flesh, the man had a charm about him. It was almost as though he wasn't going to leave Ben until he had succumbed to it.

"Beautiful place," Ben said, politely. "Is the decor your choice or your wife's?"

"My wife's no longer with us," Jagger said, in a

funeral director's tone. Having extracted a social gaffe from Ben, he strode on.

"Did you *have* to say that?" Charlene asked, in a low hiss.

"How was I to guess?" Ben said. "Did she die recently, or something?"

"How would I know?" Charlene asked. "No one talks about her."

Their conversation ended as Jagger swept back across the room. Ben recognized the "important" client who had arrived as a former cabinet minister. Roger Wellington – known in the tabloids as "Welly" – was still a backbench MP. He had a constituency near Nottingham, which probably explained why he was buying a house in the Park. Seeing the ex-minister's familiar paunch, and hearing his mellifluous voice, Ben felt vaguely nauseous, and determined to avoid conversation with the man at all costs.

Neil was fed up. He'd hated the musical, though the other three had laughed uproariously throughout it, and now he felt excluded from the conversation afterwards. The four of them sat in the Turf Tavern: him, Clare, Ruth and this guy called Steve, who was a last minute replacement for Ben. Neil knew nothing about Steve, since he'd got into the empty seat just as the show started. Steve was supposed to be with Ruth, but she had practically no conversation tonight. Neil suspected that Ruth and Ben had fallen out, but wasn't going to open that can of worms by asking about it.

Steve was one of these poncy, long-haired student types who acted like they knew it all. He had two days' worth of stubble on his chin. But what really naffed Neil off was the amount of attention Clare was giving to him. She was lapping up his stories about bands he'd seen, film directors he liked and so on. She'd obviously met him before – with Ruth, presumably. Was Ruth playing some kind of double game: seeing Steve on the side just as Ben was seeing Charlene? Did Ruth know about Charlene now? Neil couldn't understand how two people could treat each other that way.

At last, Ruth was in the loo and Steve had gone to buy a round of drinks. Neil had Clare to himself for a minute or two.

"I'm looking forward to seeing your new place tonight," he said, warmly.

Clare's face fell.

"Actually, I don't think it's a good idea if you come back tonight," she said.

"Why?"

"I've been trying to work up to telling you…"

He had one of those sinking feelings, like she was about to chuck him again. It wouldn't be the first time, or the second. He sometimes felt like he was clinging on to this relationship by his fingertips.

Then he read her expression. She was suppressing a smile.

"What is it?"

"I've got some overtime tomorrow. I'm working as an aide ... to CID."

Neil knew what working as an aide meant. The pieces of the picture slotted together. He couldn't believe it. He'd hoped that his joining CID would turn Clare on, make her want him more. Instead, it had only inspired her to go one better.

"How'd you swing that?" he asked, as though he were pleased.

"This arsonist. He – or she – burnt down half of my old school. They might be a student or ex-student. And I've worked the school before, of course, in the Hannah Brown case. People there trust me."

"I see." Neil paused for thought. "But why are you working tomorrow?"

"The sergeant I'm working with has this theory about the fires. There've been three so far, at regular intervals. The school, a bank, a factory. He thinks that there's going to be another one tomorrow."

"A serial arsonist?"

"Something like that."

"This sergeant. Who is he?"

"His name's Dylan. Do you know him?"

Neil's face fell.

"What is it?" Clare asked. "Don't you like him?"

"Oh, he's a great bloke," Neil told her. "In fact, he's going to be my tutor officer from a week on Monday."

Clare shook her head in disbelief. Steve came back with the drinks.

"Maybe the case will be resolved by then," she said.

"I certainly hope so."

"Talking shop?" Steve asked, putting a pineapple juice in front of Neil, who was driving, and giving Clare her half of lager.

"Sorry," Clare said, and started talking about French film directors again.

Half an hour later, they were out of the pub, and walking back towards Ruth and Neil's respective cars. Steve was walking with them. It took some doing, but Neil managed to separate Clare off, so that he could talk to her alone.

"You can't have to get up that early," he said. "I thought that part of your moving away from your mum and dad's was so that we could have more time … you know, alone. Do you know how little time we've spent together lately?"

Clare didn't reply directly.

"If you really want to know, I'm going to the nine o'clock service at the cathedral, then straight on to meet DS Dylan. I could maybe meet you later in the day, but I can't promise."

Neil had noticed the way Clare often slipped in a

reference to her religion when she thought he was going to try and pressure her into having sex. But he'd been more patient about that than any other guy he knew would have been. Still, there was no point in making a big deal about it. She would only get bad-tempered.

They came to Ruth's car first. Ruth had arrived earlier than Neil and parked nearer to the theatre. To Neil's surprise, Steve got in first.

"If Ruth's giving Steve a lift," Neil said to Clare, "perhaps you'd rather I drove you home."

"Don't be silly," Clare said, kissing Neil lightly on the lips before getting into the passenger seat. "Steve lives with us."

Neil watched as the three of them drove off, up and over the hill, to the house which he was excluded from.

The food finished, and having drunk slightly more wine than he'd intended to, Ben stood in a corner of Jagger's conservatory while the former minister made conversation with Charlene. Unlike other men in the room, Welly didn't use the opportunity to inspect Charlene's cleavage. The first chance he got, Ben was going to suggest that they leave. One of the younger couples had gone already, making noises about the babysitter, so he and Charly wouldn't be the first.

The ex-minister was starting to ask how Charlene

spent her spare time. He was, Ben could tell, used to success with women, even though he was fat, fifty-something and wore a wedding ring.

"Most of my spare time's spoken for by Ben here," Charlene said, in her sweetest, most hypocritical voice.

Wellington suddenly became aware of Ben, and turned to him.

"And what do you do, Ben?"

"I'm a police officer."

"Really?" The MP smiled at him. "I used to be at the Home Office."

"I know."

He was one of the idiots, Ben recalled, who reclassified various offences of criminal damage and assault so that they were no longer recorded as crimes, then boasted about a fall in the crime rate.

"What do you think of these fires we've been having, Ben? Should we worry about someone having another go at burning down the House of Commons?"

"I don't think they're political," Ben said.

"What do you think?"

"I really don't know. I'm not connected with the case."

Jagger swept by and put a hand beneath the MP's elbow.

"Excuse me. Roger. There's someone I think you ought to…"

Then, as suddenly as he'd arrived, Jagger was gone, with the former government minister following in his wake.

"OK," Charlene said. "We've spoken to both of them. We can go now."

"I don't need telling twice."

Outside, the evening was turning cool. Ben looked back at the large Victorian house, which was seemingly occupied by Jagger alone. The Park was incredibly quiet, a silence which seemed to speak of money, and the things people did to get money. Ben wanted no part of the life he'd seen tonight. Feeling emotional for a moment, he thought about Ruth. Then he got Charlene's car keys out.

"Put those away," Charly said, slipping her arm around him. "I've been counting. You've had too much to drink. And so have I. My flat's only five minutes' walk. I'll drive you home in the morning."

She leant on his shoulder as they walked back to the flat. To all the world, he and Charly looked like two young lovers enjoying a late walk in the spring air. But Ben knew that he had a decision to make. If he wasn't careful, he would make it by default. *This is what happens*, he thought. *You want the best of both worlds and you end up enjoying neither of them.*

Then, as they got into the flat, she pressed her soft body against his. Without turning the lights on, she led him into the bedroom. There was no point in fighting it, Ben decided. Charlene knew him too well. As long as she wanted him, he would come back to her.

It was as simple as that.

8

Clare overslept and didn't make early Mass. She showered quickly, then couldn't decide how to dress. What did women in CID wear? She hadn't seen enough of them to have any kind of picture in her head. All she knew was this: they dressed better than their male counterparts, but not much. In the end, she chose a tartan skirt and a pale grey blouse, which went with the black jacket she had worn to her brother's funeral. She put on her plainest tights and a pair of black court shoes. Then she changed her mind about the shoes and replaced them with her Doc Martens with the yellow stitching. She didn't want to look a complete frump.

DS Dylan wasn't there when she arrived. Clare couldn't go into the CID room without him and had to hang around by the coffee machine, wishing she'd bought a Sunday paper. Ten minutes later he showed up, wearing a garish, multicoloured jumper too thick for the season, his hair in thick clumps like he'd washed but not combed and dried it.

"Sorry I'm late. I'd promised to take the kids swimming. It's hard to make them get changed to a deadline."

"No problem."

The room was white, with clusters of desks belonging to each shift. Each desk had a couple of admin trays and two blue phones with wires which went up to the ceiling, so that it was easy to pass the handset around. There were keyboards and monitors available for each shift. In Clare's parade room, they were still sharing typewriters. On the wall at the back were large maps with see-through film over them. On the film, TWOCs were marked in green, burglaries in blue, and the suspected arsons in red. To the right of the map was a blank space.

"They used to have nudie calendars up there," Dylan told Clare. "Until the Flying Squad from Equal Opportunities made us bin them."

Not sure if this was a joke, Clare ignored the comment and made one of her own.

"It's a bit of a long shot, isn't it, guessing that there's going to be another fire today?"

"Long shots sometimes hit the target," Dylan asserted.

"But we're only talking about three fires. All right. There was a gap of three days between each of them, but that's probably coincidence."

Dylan shook his head.

"Not three fires. Four. The factory, the bank, the school, and the nightclub."

Clare was confused.

"I didn't hear about the nightclub."

Clare saw now that there were four red flags on the map. The extra one was in Beeston, well off her patch.

"Name of the place is Ciro's," Dylan explained. "The reason you didn't hear about it is that the club didn't burn down. A passer-by spotted the flames and the fire brigade got to it before much serious damage was done."

"What happened?" Clare asked.

"Club closed at two on Friday morning, sixteen days ago. The last members of staff left at two-thirty. A student, on the way back to one of the university halls of residence from a party, spotted smoke just before three."

"Any…" Clare was going to say "clues", but that wasn't a police word, so she improvised, "…evidence to suggest who started it and how?"

"There was a window open which a thin person could have climbed out of. The club's owner suggested that the arsonist could have hidden in the club after it closed, started the fire, then sneaked out. Beeston CID suspected that he'd set the fire himself, for the insurance. They let the investigation drop."

"Then our fires came along."

"Precisely. We put out a circular asking for fires with a similar MO." MO was short for the Latin *modus operandi* or method of operation.

"And?"

"And this landed on my desk Thursday. Better late than never."

Clare started to put everything together in her head. She thought aloud.

"Friday, Tuesday, Saturday, Wednesday – one's due today!"

"Precisely," Dylan agreed.

"There's only one problem," Clare added.

"What?"

"The fires are all set at night. We're here in the day."

DS Dylan gave a weak smile.

"We're lucky then, aren't we? He hasn't burnt anywhere down in the early morning, so…?"

"He'll do it this evening."

Dylan nodded.

"You haven't got any plans for tonight, have you?"

Clare shook her head.

"Good. Because I need you on call. Unpaid, I'm afraid, unless something happens. The overtime budget's really stretched this month."

"I see," Clare said, tetchily. "That's why you're calling in an aide who hasn't finished her probationary period yet?"

The detective sergeant smiled.

"No. I genuinely need you at Greencoat School tomorrow, too."

"So what do we do now?"

"Nothing."

"Pardon?"

"There's nothing we can do. We can't make any kind of guess as to where he's going to strike next. I've briefed you. From now on, you're on call, all the time. We can't guarantee that he won't strike in the day on a Sunday, when everything's quiet. You've got a car, haven't you?"

"I can borrow a friend's."

"All right." Dylan opened a drawer. "Here's your pager. I'd better get home myself. The kids are with my mother. They drive her mad if she has them for more than an hour."

Clare checked her watch. If she rushed across town she could get to the eleven-fifteen service and that would be one less thing to feel guilty about.

Clare hurried out of the station, and strode across the sunny city, up Maid Marion Way, round the back of the Playhouse, to St Barnabas Cathedral on Derby Road. The city was deserted. It was too early in the day for tourists to be visiting the castle. The only people about were vagrants and late worshippers like herself. Clare checked her watch as she got to the door. Twenty-five past.

Clare brushed sweat from her brow before walking through the glass doors. Sun streamed in from the right, and, for a moment, Clare didn't know what was going on. The cathedral was nearly empty. She stood in the family's usual place. The bishop walked in, with his red skull-cap. He was followed by the priests, all of them in red. Behind him came the choir, then the congregation, each clutching a crucifix, folded from a single palm leaf. This was a special service for Palm Sunday, the Sunday before Easter, when Roman Catholics renewed their dedication to Jesus and remembered his betrayal, arrest and journey to the cross.

Mum and Dad were at the back of the procession. Seeing Clare, they walked over with big smiles.

"You've dressed nicely for once," Dad said. "Makes a change."

Mum handed her a palm cross.

"I got an extra one," she said.

Clare wondered how Mum knew that she was coming. Then she realized that the cross hadn't been meant for her, but for Angelo, her baby brother. Before they could speak further, the choir began to sing in Latin. Clare felt the strange pull of the sacraments and switched her pager to "vibrate", so that it wouldn't make a sound during the service. The choir finished and the bishop spoke in his solemn, Irish voice.

"Let us pray."

Where do you find lots of books? In a library. Phoenix had thought about bookshops, too, but they tended to have better security than libraries. Libraries worried about people nicking individual books, or not returning them. They didn't expect anyone to break in. The one Phoenix had chosen was so run down that it didn't even have those electronic security gates. There couldn't be many books in it worth nicking.

Phoenix had made a second visit to the library on Saturday, just before it closed. The place was quiet, but no one looked up as Phoenix walked in and over to the far corner which offered the most cover. There was a gap at the end of an empty aisle. Phoenix hurried past Biography and Asian Languages, then squatted in the corner. It was a tight fit, but Phoenix's body crammed into the narrow gap. Phoenix pretended to be asleep, in case anyone spotted the person with the woolly hat, playing hide-and-seek like a ten-year-old kid.

As it turned out, there'd been no need to hide in so uncomfortable a place. A few minutes later, one of the assistants called out "Library's closing". The place was empty, so there was no last minute rush. The door was closed and the two women workers spent a few minutes tidying up. They talked about their children and the shopping they were going to do that afternoon. Then they had a moan about how their husbands refused to do anything interesting on Sundays, even though it was the only day that the whole family spent together. Then they switched off the lights and left, locking the door behind them. Neither of them had even looked in the aisle where Phoenix was hidden.

Phoenix squeezed back out of the gap. The library was dingy, but there was enough light to see. First, Phoenix double-checked the exit. It was a fire door which could be opened from the inside, and didn't appear to be alarmed. Next, Phoenix worked out where to start the fire for maximum effect.

Best, Phoenix decided, to build the pyre there and then. That way, even if someone spotted Phoenix entering the library tomorrow, there wouldn't be time to stop the fire. All Phoenix had to do was pour petrol over the books, toss on a match, and clear off.

Phoenix started with newspapers and magazines, then put on paperbacks, figuring that they would catch quicker than hardbacks. The library was near the Forest, where, every November 5th, the city put on a huge bonfire and firework display. Phoenix wanted this fire to be even bigger. The pile of books grew, stretching until they were nearly as tall as Phoenix. The fire would quickly spread to the other stacks of books. The curtains would burn. The thin wooden dividing walls would ignite. Soon, the library would be razed to the ground, just like that one in Greece, all those years ago.

Before leaving, Phoenix pulled a couple of curtains closed. Improbable that anyone could see in now, but, tomorrow, the fire shouldn't be noticed until it had had a few minutes to take hold. Finally, Phoenix got up on the chair and took the batteries out of the smoke alarm. It was tempting to start the fire there and then, but Phoenix hadn't brought the briefcase with the petrol concealed inside because it would be much safer to do it on a Sunday, when there were hardly any people around.

Now it *was* Sunday, and the area around the Forest was anything but quiet. Phoenix had left through the fire door the day before, carefully jamming an insignificant-looking bit of plastic into the lock mechanism to stop it working. It would only take a minute to do the job once the door had been kicked open. Two at most. But it was a sunny Sunday and there were lots of people around, any one of whom might clock Phoenix going into or leaving the library.

It might be sensible to come back at night, when, even if there were people watching, darkness would conceal Phoenix's appearance. But Phoenix enjoyed the challenge of setting a fire in the daylight hours, like the one at the knitwear factory. And the milk bottles full of petrol clanked reassuringly in the brown leather briefcase. All Phoenix had to do was come back a bit later. *You need patience to start a good fire.* That was what Phoenix's dad used to say, when he was huddled in front of some silly little sticks and lumps of coal, holding a newspaper in front of the grate and waiting for the coal to catch. Patience was something which Phoenix had plenty of.

Clare let herself be persuaded to go back to her parents' house for Sunday dinner. Dad promised that, if her pager went, he would drive her to the call. So they ate baked loin of lamb with peas and potatoes and plenty of gravy. Clare made conversation about her job and the family back in Italy.

"Any more interest in the house?"

The Coppola house had been on the market since December but, so far, there had been no offers.

"None," Dad said. "The agents tell us that only the cheapest houses sell. Ours is just that bit too expensive. I want to lower the price but Maria…"

"We're not giving the place away," Mum said. "That's not right. Anyway, it's spring. The estate agents say the market always picks up in the spring."

"And Neil?" Dad said. "When does he move into his new home?"

"I don't know," Clare had to admit.

"I thought it was soon. Hey, next time you come to Sunday dinner, bring him with you, won't you?"

"Maybe," Clare said. "I think it might be my turn to eat with his mum."

"Turns?" Dad said. "Who cares about turns?"

"Mrs Foster probably does," Mum said quietly. "How is she?"

"Well, as far as I know."

When they'd finished the coffee, Clare got up to go.

"I'll drive you home," Dad insisted.

"It's only a ten minute walk. I'll be fine."

"But what if your pager goes?"

"I pass at least five phone boxes. I'll use the nearest one. And I'll call a taxi or patrol car if it's necessary." She kissed her father on the cheek, then her mother too. "Thanks for dinner, Mum. It was delicious."

"Come and see us again soon."

"I will."

Clare walked back along Gregory Boulevard, hoping that the pager would go off, that something would happen before she got back to the house, where Neil was bound to have rung her. She could do with Neil being away for another week, while she thought about how things were between them.

Clare liked Neil. She respected him. She sometimes had fun with him. She cared a lot about him. But did she love him? They'd known each other for twenty-one months. They'd been going out with each other, on and off, for over a year. Perhaps,

Clare thought, you could love someone without being *in love*. She hadn't been *in love* since she was sixteen. Though there was a brief time, during her first term at university, when she thought she was.

After such a long time together, could love still come, or was that too much to ask? Clare was twenty years old. She was too young to be settling for less than she wanted. But Neil wouldn't wait for ever for Clare to commit herself, physically or mentally.

Clare walked through the centre of Hyson Green, past the carpet store and the old police station, which was now used by Social Services. The streets were quiet now. Most people would be eating or watching the live football game on the TV. Clare heard a noise, then glanced down an alleyway to her left. She saw someone – a shadowy figure in a woolly hat – darting out of a door and down the alleyway, towards the flats behind.

He had come out of the library, Clare realized, the library where she had borrowed endless books as a child. But why was he coming out of the library on a Sunday? She went after him. Half-way down the alley, the reason became apparent.

Clare heard and smelt the fire before she saw it. The air reeked of petrol. There was a kind of soft *whoosh* as the flames sprang into life. When Clare reached the fire exit, the whole thing began to go up. She saw a trail of petrol stretching from the pile of burning books in the middle to the curtains at the front. The carpet was alight and the curtains were about to go up.

The heat was strong, but nothing to what it would be once the fire really took hold. Clare ran into the library and took the extinguisher from the wall. She pointed it, pulled the lever, and foam poured out, damping down the carpet before the fire could catch the curtains. Then she turned and let the whole lot go into the pile of books, circling it thoroughly so that the foam starved the flames of oxygen. Within a minute, the fire was out.

With tears streaming from her smoke-filled eyes, Clare ran out of the building. There was no sign of the arsonist. She went to the phone and summoned the fire brigade, then got DS Dylan at home. She knew he wasn't going to be pleased.

9

"You went in to stop the fire rather than going after the culprit? You joined the wrong service, girl. You ought to be in the fire brigade!"

"I was on my own. I wouldn't have caught him, sir."

Dylan sighed.

"You might at least have got near enough to make a decent ID. Are you even sure it was a *him*?"

Clare tried to think.

"Not entirely, no. The offender had his or her back to me. He was wearing some kind of hat – one of those long wool ones, turned up – a ski hat: they're quite fashionable these days, for boys and girls. At least we know that the arsonist is young, and thin, the way I described them before."

"Think carefully – the way this person moved – was there anything else?"

Clare concentrated.

"He – or she – was carrying some kind of bag in the left hand."

"A plastic bag?"

"No. More like a case. A briefcase or … I only saw it for a moment or two, but it reminded me of one of those old-fashioned cases people used to carry sheet music in. Do you know what I mean?"

"Like a small suitcase, with squared corners?"

"Yes."

DS Dylan radioed this description in, then looked at her.

"Next time, think. All you saved were a few books. You had time to make an arrest and still stop the library burning down."

"Yes, sir."

"So far, this idiot's only endangered property, not people. But that might change."

He didn't say *and if people die, you'll be responsible*. He didn't have to. Clare had worked that out for herself.

"Go home. Have a bath. Get changed. I'll meet you at the school in the morning."

Clare did as she was told.

Ruth was on the two to ten shift, starting on Sunday afternoon. For once, she was glad to be working on a weekend. It stopped her from moping around the house, waiting for Ben to call, which he hadn't. And Sunday was a quiet day for crime: the odd domestic, break-ins at buildings which were closed for the day, and some shoplifting, now that so many stores opened on what used to be the day of rest. Ruth and Roy Tate, her tutor officer, walked around this city at rest, reassuring people by their presence.

Roy was fifty-something and easy to work with. He was still a PC and proud of his lack of ambition. There were many coppers like Roy, though most had retired by the time they got to his age. Maybe Ruth would be like that herself one day. She didn't know what she wanted from the force in the long run. It was less than a year since she'd decided to become a police officer. Before that, Ruth worked as a radio operator in her home town, Halifax. The police was just a job for her then. In some ways, it still was: a better paid, but often boring job.

She and Roy walked across the Forest, where most of the day's football games were over. Dogs were being walked. Ruth was lost in her own thoughts and only heard the message on the radio. It was a burglary in progress. A patrol car would get to it first.

"That's your street, isn't it?" Roy said.

"Yes," Ruth said, waking up. "What number did they say?"

He told her. Ruth swore. It was the house next

door. The one on the other side, which hadn't been burgled yet. Ruth and Roy began to run.

Roy was more than twice Ruth's age but he was fitter than her. She had trouble keeping up with him. When they got to the house, Ruth was out of breath and sweaty. A patrol car was at the other end of the street, negotiating its way over the speed bumps. Roy went round the back while Ruth watched the front of the house. They didn't know yet who had called them or whether an intruder was still inside the house.

"Got lost," the driver admitted as he got out of the car. Forest Fields was a maze of interweaving streets with endless restrictions to prevent cars making a rat run through them. "What's the score?"

"No idea," Ruth said. "Roy's round the back. Why don't you go after him? I'll cover the front."

He did as she suggested. Nine times out of ten, the burglar would escape from the back of the house, where he was less likely to be seen. Ruth gave it a few seconds, then rang the doorbell. She wasn't expecting anyone to answer. But the door was opened almost immediately. By Steve.

"What are you doing here?"

"Mrs Patel's in our place. She came round in a panic, said someone was in the house. Sam rang the police and then called me down."

"But what did you go inside for?" Ruth asked. "It might have been dangerous."

"Nah," Steve said, with no show of false bravado. "There's nobody here. I thought I might at least get a glimpse of the burglar, see if it's kids or whatever. But nothing."

Ruth was disappointed.

"We'd better get Mrs Patel back in," she said, "see if anything's missing."

A minute later, two of the three officers sat in the kitchen of Ruth's house.

"This is getting to be a regular police convention," Steve told them.

Sam retreated to the living-room, but Steve made a pot of tea.

"Any signs of forced entry at the back?" Ruth asked the patrol car driver.

"Everything was locked up tight."

"How did you get in?" she asked Steve.

"Mrs P. left the front door open."

Then Roy came in with Mrs Patel.

"Once a month we spend Sunday afternoon at my sister-in-law's," Mrs Patel explained. "But I forgot to bring the video camera. My husband was going to make a little film showing all the family, you understand? But when I went in to get it, I heard a noise, upstairs. So I came in here and Sam called the police."

"Do you think the burglar heard you?" Ruth asked. "Did you call out?"

"No. I opened the door. That was all. I was only

in the house for a few seconds."

"And what have they taken?"

"Nothing. The video camera was on the dining-room table, where we left it. The TV, my jewels ... everything is there."

"Look," Roy said to Mrs Patel in a reassuring voice. "I know there've been a lot of burglaries on this street and it's worrying everybody. But noises travel easily in terraced houses like these. There's no sign of a break-in. You probably heard someone moving around in another house and thought it was a burglar upstairs. It's an easy enough mistake to make."

"I know what I heard!" Mrs Patel protested. "There was someone upstairs, moving things about."

"Was anything in the wrong position?" Ruth asked.

"I can't be sure."

"Maybe when the rest of the family comes back, if anything's lost or missing, we can look into this again," Roy continued. "But, at the moment, there's no evidence for us to record this as an attempted burglary. I'm sorry."

"Why don't you go back to your family party?" Ruth suggested. "Whatever happened, there's no need to let it spoil your day."

Mrs Patel did as Ruth suggested. The patrol driver left.

"You've got the attic room," Ruth said to Steve. "Did you hear anything suspicious?"

" 'Fraid not."

"Or was anyone in our house moving about – could that have been what Mrs Patel heard?"

Steve shrugged apologetically.

"Dunno. I was playing music. Sam had to shout really loud to get me downstairs."

"Come on," Roy said. "Time to get on."

"Quite a day you two are having," Steve said, as they got up to go.

"Us two?"

"You with imaginary burglaries and Clare with her burning books."

"What books?" Ruth asked.

Steve told her. Ruth was impressed. That was Clare for you, casually putting out a fire on her way home from dinner.

"Is she in?" Ruth asked.

Steve shook his head.

"She had a bath, then that bloke, Neil, came round and picked her up." He paused, then added, "Tell me something."

"What?"

"How long has she been going out with him?"

"About a year. Why?"

So he *was* interested in Clare. Ruth wasn't surprised.

"He doesn't seem like her type. That's all."

"You never know about people," Ruth replied. "Do you?"

* * *

Phoenix was angry. Talk about bad luck. Some girl comes along and calmly puts out the fire. Another minute, and she wouldn't have been able to get into the place for the heat. Phoenix was tempted to find another library, burn it down, but that would be a panic measure. It wouldn't be so bad if that letter hadn't gone off to the media.

There was only one way to get around it. The next one would have to be big: really big. Something which made people sit up and take notice. Something which would put the name of Phoenix on to the front pages and into the history books. National news.

Maybe the best bet would be to finish after the next big one. And then that would be it. Over. The mistake most criminals made, they didn't know when to stop. They went on too long and got caught. Not Phoenix. Some time soon, Phoenix's career would end.

With a bang.

10

Miss Thornber escorted Clare to one of the Portakabins which had been brought in to replace burnt-out classrooms. The two women knew each other. Miss Thornber once taught Clare geography. She had also been Clare's brother's form teacher until his death.

School didn't start for twenty minutes, but, already, children were milling round, gaping at the scaffolding and canvas which covered the shell of what had once been the school hall.

"When will they rebuild?" Clare asked.

"Not until the summer holidays. Easter's too close and in the wrong financial year to get anything done. So we're stuck with this for a term. And this week's going to be hell. There's only a week to go before the holiday. If you ask me, they should have kept the school closed this week as well."

"I'm glad they didn't," Clare said as they sat down in the makeshift classroom. "With over four weeks off, the trail would be completely cold." The walls of the Portakabin were bare but Miss Thornber had two potted plants on her desk, giving the room some personality.

"What do you hope to find out?" the teacher asked.

"We need to establish whether the arsonist here was a one off, or is responsible for some of the other fires in the city."

"The radio today said something about a library fire caused by a phoenix," Miss Thornber commented. "Is that part of what you're talking about?"

"I don't know," Clare said, confused. "Maybe."

Clare hadn't listened to the radio news that morning. The library fire wasn't big enough to make yesterday's bulletins, though. Had there been another one? And what had a phoenix to do with it? A familiar voice interrupted her thoughts.

"Hey, Clare! What are you doing here?"

Hannah Brown had cut her hair shorter, in a style which didn't flatter her. Otherwise, she looked about a hundred times better than when Clare had last seen her, as a teenage runaway.

"Investigating fires. How are you?"

"I'm great. You look well. Is there anything I can do to help?"

"Depends whether you've heard anything."

Hannah shook her head.

"Not in the last week. I've been revising. But you know what schools are like. There'll be a rumour mill the size of the Forest ground by lunchtime."

Clare got out her notebook.

"If you hear anything – no matter how small, or ludicrous – let me know. I'll give you my number."

"I've already got it," Hannah reminded her.

"I've moved," Clare said, as she handed her the slip of paper.

"Really? Are you living with that guy, the one in the car chase? What was his name?"

"Neil. No, I'm not living with him. With friends."

Clare didn't need reminding about Neil. Her boyfriend had a completion date on his house: the Tuesday after Easter. Yesterday, against her better judgement, she'd agreed to help him move into the small house in Carrington. The house was close to her new home: too close, if Clare finally decided to finish with him.

"Know a boy called Scott James?" Clare asked Hannah.

"Everyone knows Scott. He's in the year below me. A right wally."

"In what way?"

"Silly. A loudmouth. Bullies younger children. That kind of thing."

"You don't think he's the type to start a fire?"

"He's stupid enough to. But not clever enough to make a success of it."

"Thanks," Clare told Hannah. "Please don't mention to anyone that I was asking about him. I don't want to feed the rumour mill myself."

The door opened and they went quiet. But it wasn't another student. It was DS Dylan.

"Sorry I'm late," he said. "Can we talk somewhere alone?"

Hannah escorted them to the small interview room which the Head was allowing CID to use.

"What is it?" Clare asked when they were inside.

"I take it you haven't heard the radio news this morning?"

'No. But a teacher just mentioned something … about a phoenix?'

Dylan nodded and handed Clare a sheet of thermal paper.

"Radio Nottingham faxed us this as soon as they got it. Trent and the *Post* were sent one too. Forensic are getting hold of the originals, but I'll be surprised if they tell us anything more than the make of typewriter."

Clare read the letter.

"He doesn't say *which* library, or even that it is a library. It wouldn't have done much good, even if we'd seen the letter before the fire."

Dylan agreed.

"It was posted at five on Saturday afternoon. We

weren't meant to get it until after the fire. This arsonist is interested in getting credit."

"The rubber stamp is unusual," Clare said. "What about the name, *Phoenix*?"

"I'm told it comes from an abandoned egg which cracks open in the fire. A phoenix is the bird which rises from the flames. Not terribly original."

"As I recall, Mars is the god of fire," Clare said, "but the name doesn't sound as good, does it? He'd be known as the *Mars bar* man."

Dylan laughed.

"You know a bit about mythology. Not many people do these days."

"There's this RE teacher at the school – Mrs Wain – she used to do all that myths and legends stuff."

Dylan smiled.

"That kind of knowledge is exactly why I want you here."

Clare saw what he was getting at.

"You still think that this Phoenix could be a student at the school?"

"Or an ex-student. Have you picked up anything so far this morning?"

"I've only spoken to two people. I did enquire about a boy called Scott James."

Dylan checked his notebook.

"Yes. He was interviewed at your suggestion. But not by me. By my oppo. Ken's been transferred to

Trent Division. New lad doesn't start till next week."

Clare didn't mention that she knew who Dylan's new trainee was to be.

"Did James have an alibi?"

"Claimed to be in bed at the time. Mother supported him. No previous, unless you count a caution for spraying his name on the wall of the primary school he used to go to. He's small fry."

"Not so small," Clare said. "He's tall and thin, same as the guy I saw on both occasions."

"Point taken," Dylan said. "I'll interview him when I'm working my way through the boys. Are you ready to start on the girls?"

Clare nodded.

"OK. I'll take this room. You find somewhere else."

"Yes, sir."

"And when school's over, I want you to go into town, see if you can find the shop which sold that rubber stamp, or whatever it is."

"You'd better give me that fax," Clare pointed out.

"Pick up a copy of the *Evening Post*. It'll be on the front cover."

"Publicity's all the arsonist needs," Clare complained. "Can't we stop them?"

Dylan shook his head.

"Stop them publishing a letter which was sent to

their paper? Hardly. Close the door on your way out, would you? There's a draught."

Typical, Clare thought. You find the one decent space in the school to talk in and the senior officer bags it. The school was overcrowded – even more so, after the fire. She would have to use a changing-room, or a corner of the kitchens.

Clare had been at the school since eight. When she was done, she would have to charge into town and go round the shops until they closed at six. She'd get no lunchtime worth speaking of, and there'd be no overtime pay for the extra two hours she'd worked. Serve her right for expecting detective work to be glamorous.

In the corridor Clare spotted a familiar face, waiting to be interviewed. It was Carol Ward, who used to deliver papers with Angelo. They greeted each other.

"This room's occupied. I need another free space to interview people. Any ideas?"

Carol thought for a minute.

"There's the video editing room. It used to be the school dark room, so it's very small."

"Can you fit two chairs in there?"

"Just about."

"It'll do. Who'd have a key?"

"Miss Greenwood. I'll take you to her."

Clare borrowed a piece of paper from the girl's rough book and pinned a note to the door. Then she set off for another round of interviews which, Clare knew, were almost certain to be a complete waste of time.

Inspector Grace summoned Jan into his office. This was a routine weekly meeting. Or so Jan thought. The inspector was playing with a pencil, nervously, and didn't meet Jan's eyes. They had been working together for nearly six months now. Jan was coming to the conclusion that Grace wasn't comfortable with women.

Grace was small, for a policeman. Not bad-looking, but there was something weasel-like about him. He dressed well. Surprising, then, that he was unmarried. Most policemen seemed to marry young. Maybe he was gay. But gay men usually got on well with women. Or so Jan had heard. She didn't know any herself.

Truth was, Jan resented Grace. He was younger than her – she'd never dared ask, but he was in his late twenties at most – ridiculously young for an inspector. She'd been proud to make sergeant by thirty. And Grace lived for his work, while Jan had a family, so her family came first.

Which, as it turned out, was what he wanted to talk to her about.

"You know my commitment to equal oppor- tunities," Grace began by saying. Jan nodded. It was only a few weeks since he'd practically forced her to go on a "race awareness" course.

"That commitment extends to women officers with children returning to the workplace."

"Good."

"However…"

Jan knew the sound of that "however". It was the sound of a plug being pulled out of a bath.

"There have been numerous instances of poor timekeeping recently, sergeant. You're late more often than you're on time."

"That isn't true, I…"

From the way Grace's eyes narrowed Jan knew better than to interrupt any further.

"You've taken time off to deal with your child's illnesses – understandable, of course, but I have to question the cost. We're way over budget on over-time and much of that is down to extra officers covering you." He paused. Jan considered her reply carefully. But Grace hadn't finished yet.

"We're a team. We support each other when we're having difficulties. I hope you feel that we've given every support to you…"

"Yes, sir."

"But that commitment works both ways. It's been noted, for instance, that you leave the station almost the moment your shift is over. This makes briefing the incoming shift less thorough than it ought to be. It also has an effect on your shift's morale."

Jan couldn't hold back any longer.

"I don't think that's fair, sir. There are times, of course, when I'm juggling childcare arrangements and have to leave quickly, or barely arrive on time. Last week, for instance, my childminder was ill, and I had to—"

"I don't want to hear this,' Grace interrupted. "I repeat. We make allowances for your being a parent – concessions, even. But you do have to sort out an efficient childcare system. And when we're talking about equal opportunities, it's not unreasonable to expect your husband to make an equal contribution."

Didn't he think she'd tried?

"My husband works even more ridiculous shifts than I do," Jan explained.

"I'm sure his employers would be as under-standing as we are."

Jan sighed. Kevin was a junior hospital registrar. Grace had obviously never met a National Health Service Trust Fund manager.

"It's somewhat harder for men to get leave for childcare, sir. Can you imagine Tim or John missing work to look after their kids?"

Grace frowned.

"If they asked, I would, of course, do my best to help. But we're talking about you. I'm also not satisfied with your shift's paperwork. The returns are the worst of the five shifts I manage. You're behind in your weekly reports and some of the case notes I'm seeing are getting sloppy."

"We're badly understaffed. But I'll get it sorted."

"The understaffing was my final point. What I'm seeing, sergeant, are the results of poor morale. This month, you've lost two of your most promising officers, one of them permanently."

Interesting to know that Clare Coppola was classed as a most promising officer, but Jan didn't comment on that.

"I'll be sorry if Neil stays in CID but it's a good career move – hardly a sign of low morale."

"Maybe. I'm trying to sort out a replacement for him as quickly as possible."

"Thank you."

Jan tried not to glance at her watch. It was nearly two. Kevin had to make a ward round at half past so she needed to be back to look after Henry. Had Grace finished? He seemed to have. He was playing with his pencil again. Jan stood.

"I'll try to improve the situation, sir."

Best to eat humble pie. Grace stood too. She was taller than him. He couldn't like that. She was taller than Neil, too, but he was her inferior.

"If you want to transfer to a less onerous job with more regular hours," Grace said, "I'll give you every assistance possible."

Jan flinched. She'd thought she was just getting a bollocking, but he was trying to push her out.

"I want to do real police work, sir."

"It's all real. I'm sure you know that."

"I'm happy with what I'm doing."

Grace's expression had no more compassion than a stone. Jan tensed up.

"Was this a formal reprimand, sir? Because if it was, I think I might need to consult my federation rep, to see exactly where I stand."

"It wasn't a formal reprimand," Grace said, quietly. "Not this time."

He held the door open for her to leave.

11

The suspect sneered at Neil, then repeated, "You're joking, right? This is a fit-up."

"We found the gun at your house," Neil said, for the fourth time. "If you didn't put it there, who did?"

"The police, that's who!"

"Listen," Neil said. "If I got caught planting a gun on a toerag like you, I'd be out of the force faster than you can finish smoking that cigarette. Get my point? You aren't worth it. So where did you get that gun?"

The suspect paused. For a moment, Neil was sure that he was going to ask for a lawyer. Then he stubbed his cigarette out and came up with a new answer.

"Found it, dinni?"

Neil began to relax a little.

"Now we're getting somewhere."

When the interview was over, Neil took the tape and immediately wrote it up. Making an accurate transcript took more than twice as long as the original interview lasted. He handed his paperwork in and waited for the verdict.

The debriefing, when it came, was surprisingly thorough. Neil felt like his performance was being taken to pieces. The training officer hardly referred to Neil's notes. Instead, he showed Neil himself on video.

"Your body language is too confrontational. Look at yourself. You're meant to be building a rapport with the interviewee. How do you appear?"

"Spiky."

"Precisely. Lean back now and then. Learn to smile. Establish eye contact. Crack a joke. The interviewee will find it harder to lie to you."

After ten minutes of this, the training officer picked up the report.

"Well written. Only one spelling mistake. Very accurate to the tapes. This would stand up in court one hundred percent." Neil was beginning to smile when the officer added, "A pity, though, that your interview technique was so pathetic. The suspect had in his possession a gun which had been used to kill a police officer. All you managed to establish was a ludicrous story about how he'd found the gun by a riverbank, where someone had tried to throw it in, but missed!"

Neil tried to stand up for himself.

"But the stupidity of the story would help to convict him. He was hardly going to give himself up for shooting an officer, was he?"

"Not deliberately, no. But there were four separate points in the interview where the suspect contradicted himself or mentioned details which you failed to pick up on. Any one of these might have led to his story coming apart – if you'd spotted them."

By the end of the debriefing, Neil felt thoroughly humiliated. What was he doing training for CID? People said it all the time: you either had the stuff to be a detective, and any other career was a failure, or you didn't, in which case you were wasting everybody's time. Neil didn't think he had it.

Dejected, he tried to ring Clare. It was just after six, but the guy who answered the phone, Steve, said she wasn't back from work yet. She must be on a 3-11 instead of a 9-5. He felt hurt that she hadn't told him.

Clare traipsed round the city, wondering what she'd let herself in for. None of the stationers she'd been into sold rubber stamps of any but the most basic kind.

"Could be hand-made," said the man in Pensense.

"Can you think of anywhere which might have sold it?" Clare asked.

"There's a specialist rubber stamp shop in Amsterdam," the man told her. "And another in Los Angeles. But Nottingham? I think Tokenhouse do a few. Have you tried there?"

"Not yet," Clare said. "Thanks."

In Tokenhouse they told her to try Yellow Pages. Clare had already done that. There were several companies listed who made rubber stamps. Not surprisingly, none of them had made up one of a phoenix rising in recent memory. This arsonist wasn't stupid. He or she would have bought a ready-made one – or made it themselves – in which case, Clare had no chance of finding them.

Clare had run out of shops. She walked past St Peter Chambers, down to King John's Arcade, intending to cut through there to the Market Square. Then she saw a shop she hadn't noticed before: Tableworks. It looked like an upmarket Habitat, with lots of vases, crockery and handmade furniture. But it was just possible that...

Clare walked in two minutes before the shop closed and asked if they sold rubber stamps. They were right by the side of the counter – about twenty of them, in a box. They had Thank Yous, noughts and crosses, teddy bears, flowers, the sun and moon. But no phoenix. Clare showed the picture in the newspaper to the teenage girl behind the till.

"Have you ever sold a stamp like this one?"

She shrugged.

"Maybe. If it's not in the box, we don't have it."

"I don't want to buy one. I want to know if you've sold one."

"We're closing now."

Clare got out her warrant card. The assistant called the owner from the back.

"Is this familiar?" Clare asked the red-haired woman.

"It *could* be one of ours."

"You don't remember selling one?"

"I'm sorry. These little wooden blocks are very popular. I check the boxes to restock them every so often, but I wouldn't generally look at one when we sell it – just check the price."

"Do you know of anywhere else that sells these?"

"Not in the East Midlands."

Clare thought for a moment.

"When you reorder them, is there some sort of catalogue that you use?"

"Why, yes. Would you like to see it?"

The catalogue contained two thousand illustrations of all shapes and sizes. Clare's brain was tired and the two women watching her flick through it were showing signs of impatience. Clare was about to ask if she could borrow the catalogue when one of the images leapt off the page at her.

"Have you any way of checking if you've ever had this one in stock?"

"I'd have to go right through the order books. Is this really necessary?"

Clare wasn't sure.

"I need to establish if the stamp was bought here…"

"It couldn't have been bought anywhere else."

"…and then whether anyone saw it being bought. How many other staff do you have?"

"Three. And my husband. Two of them only work on Saturdays. I'll give you their details."

"Can I go now?" the assistant asked as the manager wrote down the addresses.

"Yes. Fine."

This was a long shot, Clare realized. People who worked in shops rarely remembered individual customers, unless they did something out of the ordinary. The assistant put on her coat.

"Wouldn't you be better off just taking the videos?" the assistant asked, as she unlocked the shop door.

"Videos?"

The owner pointed at the camera on the ceiling.

"It's on all the time, in case we need evidence against shoplifters."

Clare knew what it was for. She was kicking herself for not having noticed it earlier.

"How far back do the tapes go?"

"A week. Then we reuse them. Do you want to take some?"

An hour later, Clare found herself in the living-room at home, watching well-heeled browsers inspecting vases, picture frames and table lamps. She should probably be doing this at work, but Clare had several more school kids to interview and forty-eight hours of tape to view. If the arsonist had had the stamp for ages, or had even bought it last Monday, he was safe. But if not...

There were three cameras, covering every part of the store. Everybody who came in was caught on videotape. It was mind-numbingly boring to watch. Clare put on a soul compilation tape which Neil had made for her. It helped her to concentrate. She sang along with Luther Vandross on "Searching" as someone selected a candlestick. She duetted with Gladys Knight on "Midnight Train to Georgia" as a middle-aged man pocketed a picture frame without paying for it, unnoticed by the assistant, who was being chatted up by a delivery boy.

As Clare harmonized with the Blue Notes on Howard Melvin's "If you don't know me by now", the door opened.

"Having a party?" Steve asked.

"Believe it or not," Clare told him, "I'm working." She explained.

"I'm half-way through the first of twelve four-hour tapes," she finished.

"Can't you fast-forward it?" Steve suggested.

She shook her head.

"It's easy enough to miss something as it is."

"Have you seen what time it is?"

Clare realized that it was nearly ten. She'd been working without a break for fourteen hours.

"Come on," Steve said. "Take a break. Let me buy you a drink."

"You twisted my arm," Clare told him.

Steve looked lazily sexy in his flying jacket. Clare felt good walking into the Carlton with him, in a way she wouldn't if it was Neil by her side. Neil made her feel like a policewoman. There were certain places where they didn't fit. As Steve bought the drinks, Clare wondered where he got his money. The dole didn't go far and Steve had been on it for ten months. Maybe his family had money. Or maybe he had something going on the side. Once, Clare would have objected to that, but police work taught you about poverty. People did what they had to do to get by and if it didn't hurt anyone, what was the problem?

"It was good of you to go round to Mrs Patel's the other day," she said, as Steve sat down. He looked embarrassed.

"It was nothing."

"Nothing? You might have run into someone. You didn't have a weapon. You might have got hurt. That takes guts."

"You suggesting I'd make a good recruit?" Steve asked, with a twinkle in his eye.

"There are good prospects for graduates," Clare said.

They both laughed. No way would Steve fit into the police culture.

"Well," Clare corrected herself, "I bet you'd be good undercover in the Drugs Squad."

"If I could keep my hands off the evidence."

Clare smiled and their eyes met. They were flirting. Steve wasn't straight, and that was part of what attracted her to him. But did Clare's job turn Steve on or put him off? She didn't have long to find out.

They walked home with bodies casually brushing against each other. The house was empty. They stood in the hallway, still so close that they were almost touching.

"Let's go up to my room," Steve suggested, "get comfortable."

Clare hesitated. She knew that if she went upstairs, she would not be able to put Steve off, the way she kept putting Neil off. She wasn't even sure if she'd want to.

"I don't think my boyfriend would understand," Clare replied, as lightly as she could. It was the first time she'd referred to Neil that evening.

"All right," Steve said. "But the offer stays open. OK?"

Clare gave him a regretful smile.

"OK."

He kissed her on the forehead and walked quickly upstairs, not giving Clare time to change her mind.

12

"You're not a lawyer, you're a crook!"

An untidy man with wild eyes crashed out of Ian Jagger's office, pulling his jacket around his shoulders but failing to put it on properly. The effect was comic, as though the man were attempting to get out of a strait-jacket. But Charlene wasn't laughing. Jagger stood behind the man, his voice conciliatory and calm.

"You have, of course, every right to change your solicitors, Mr Benson. If you give us written notice, I'll have a secretary make up your bill. Then, when it's paid, we'll happily transfer the files to your new lawyers."

"You know where you can go!" the man called Benson yelled. "You're all in it together, you lot.

You hear me? You're the thieves!"

He wrestled an arm free from the jacket, pulled the door open and charged down the corridor into the street. Jagger shook his head slowly, then, seeing Charlene watching him, gave a sad smile. Charlene raised her eyebrows sympathetically. All solicitors got their share of loonies.

"He's about to lose his business," Jagger explained. "It gets people that way sometimes."

"He expected you to save him?"

Jagger shrugged.

"I've been trying to help him reschedule his debts. Technically, it's not our job. But a lot of people are suing him for bills he hasn't paid. It's the usual story. He's actually owed more than he owes, but he can't get paid quickly enough. He's got no cash flow and the bank pulled the plug on him. It's up to the receivers now."

"Sad."

Jagger agreed.

"What's also sad is that we'll be the last people to get paid. But never mind that."

He looked over Charlene's shoulder at the brief she was preparing. It was for an assault case later in the week.

"Busy?"

"I'm on top of it," Charlene asserted.

"Good. Let me take you to lunch. It's about time we talked properly."

Charlene hesitated for a moment. Going to Jagger's house was one thing. Going to lunch with him alone was another. She had yet to be convinced by Ben's allegations against the lawyer. However, that didn't mean she trusted him. He was, perhaps, too charming. But Ian Jagger was already putting on his jacket, taking her acceptance for granted. And he was her boss. She followed him out.

Charlene and Jagger walked across the city to Sonny's, a posh restaurant in Hockley. The staff there seemed to know the lawyer. Even so, the service was slow, and they had plenty of time to talk. Away from the office, Charlene found, Jagger was a good listener. She told him about her aspirations in the job. He was encouraging about the kind of cases she would soon be allowed to handle.

"Did you enjoy the party on Saturday?" her boss asked, when they'd finished their starters.

"Eh, yes. Some of the company was a bit ... over-whelming."

"You'll soon get used to that kind of society," Jagger assured her. "You know what they say: the rich are the same as the rest of us – they just have more money."

Charlene laughed.

"And your boyfriend, did he have a good time?"

"I think so."

"Roger mentioned that he's in the police."

"That's right."

"An unusual alliance, for a solicitor."

"Is it?"

Charlene changed the subject.

"So Roger Wellington's bought a house in the Park?"

"An apartment, yes."

"I didn't see his wife there on Saturday. Is she well?"

Wellington was one of those politicians who was often pictured with his family. Charlene remembered a motherly, grey-haired woman, a rosy-cheeked teenage daughter.

"She won't be living with him."

Charlene gulped. She'd put her foot in it.

"They've been living separate lives for many years. Now that Roger's no longer in government, and their daughter's left home, he and Hilary are going to quietly divorce. That's why Roger's bought a Nottingham base in the Park – not too far from the constituency, not too near Hilary."

"I see."

"In fact," Jagger pointed out, "his new place is very near to you."

Charlene wasn't sure if her boss was trying to tell her something. She finished her baked salmon.

"Can I interest you in dessert?" Jagger asked, with a fatherly smile.

"Shouldn't we be getting back to work?" Charlene said.

"If you insist."

Charlene tried to pay half the bill but her boss wouldn't let her.

"Next time," he said.

Charlene wasn't sure if he meant next time she could pay for lunch or next time she could pay half. But it definitely meant that they would be having lunch together again. She hadn't noticed Jagger lunching with the other solicitors who worked for him. She was in favour. Best, she decided, as they walked through Slab Square towards Jagger's, not to tell Ben about the lunch. He wouldn't understand.

"You can watch the videos if you like," Dylan told Clare as the bell went for the end of school. "But it'll be in your own time. Think about it. The rubber stamp could've been bought anywhere, any time. Even if it was bought at Tableworks last week, the chances are that the camera won't have picked up the person buying it. And the things are tiny. How will you be able to tell that the person on the video is buying a stamp with the Phoenix motif on it?"

"Maybe I'll recognize him," Clare suggested. "After all, I've seen the arsonist twice."

"Sure. In silhouette and from behind. Now, tell me, did you learn anything this morning?"

Clare shook her head.

"One girl mentioned Scott James — yet again —

said he'd been mouthing off about the fire. But she didn't think that he'd actually done it. By the way, did we get any further with the library?"

Dylan shook his head.

"We've contacted most of the people who were in the library on Saturday morning. No one saw anything suspicious – certainly not a tall thin person with a woolly hat who smelt of petrol."

"I've got a feeling," Clare said.

"What?"

"I think we're wasting our time at the school. If anyone was going to tell us anything, they'd have told us by now. Meanwhile, our Phoenix is getting ready to set another fire on Thursday."

"Which," Dylan said, "is precisely why we're going to stick at the school until Thursday. Maybe we'll discover something. Maybe our presence will put the arsonist off from doing whatever he's going to do next."

"Presuming," Clare said, "that he goes to this school. I've got a feeling he doesn't."

Dylan frowned.

"Detective work, officer, isn't about having *feelings*, it's about thorough, methodical investigation."

"Point taken," Clare said. She added, hopefully, "Are you going to need me beyond Thursday?"

"Too soon to say."

"It's just that I'm meant to be on nights from

Sunday," Clare explained. "Friday and Saturday are my rest days."

"I'll tell you what," Dylan said.

"What?"

He smiled benignly.

"I'll let you take Saturday off. The rest of the week you can work your shift at nights and for me during the day."

"Ha ha," Clare said, before realizing that he was serious.

"It's good for the character," Dylan said, "working to the limits of your endurance. It's how you tell the women from the girls."

"I can think of better ways," Clare told him, with a withering look. "Now I'm going home to look through my videos."

She expected him to make a sarcastic comment, or insist that she work on until five. Instead, Dylan nodded and said, "Good luck!" as she opened the door. Clare reckoned she'd need it.

Phoenix read through the headlines with pleasure. Somehow, the failure of the library fire hadn't spoilt the story.

"SERIAL ARSONIST STRIKES AGAIN!" screamed the *Post*.

"Self-proclaimed *Phoenix* writes exclusively to us."

The attention was gratifying. It was almost

tempting to carry on beyond the next one, to keep going until caught, then go out in a blaze of publicity…

But no, Phoenix decided against. Once you were caught, that was it. You went to gaol. You didn't pass "go". You never got the chance to do it again. Far better to retire undefeated. Then, in years to come, who knew? A comeback. All Phoenix had to do was hold on to the stamp, which was like a fingerprint, or signature. No two were the same. Phoenix would be the sort of celebrity whose myth grew over the years, like Jack the Ripper. He was never caught. Nor was his real identity ever revealed. That kind of fame would be satisfying. Though it would be even more satisfying to let just one person know who the Phoenix really was – a person who couldn't do anything about it.

Where next? There was a place on the edge of the city, a business park called The Phoenix Centre. But that was too big and obvious a target. There was an Arts centre in Leicester which was also called the Phoenix and would be easier to burn down – perhaps too easy. No. Phoenix would prefer to stick to the city of Nottingham. If this was to be the final fire, it had to be something spectacular, something photogenic.

What burnt better than anything else? The answer to the question was so obvious that Phoenix almost leapt for joy.

13

Five days. Ruth hadn't seen or heard from Ben for five days. All she did was mope about. She'd been meaning to decorate her room, but couldn't work up the energy. After work, she tried to unwind with the TV, but it rarely worked. She slept badly, when she slept at all. Her old flat was in a quiet cul-de-sac. Here, the night was full of noises, real and imagined.

It had been days since the last burglary. If a burglar was working his way down the street, he must have decided to give this place a miss. It made sense to miss number twenty-one, because the occupants kept such irregular hours. You could never be sure who was home. Tonight, though, the house was empty, and in darkness. As Ruth let herself in, the phone was ringing. Ruth hurried to it, hoping that it would be Ben. But the caller hung up just as she got to it.

Ruth rang British Telecom. They had a service which told you the number of the last person who'd called. If it *was* Ben, she could call him back. But it wasn't. Ruth didn't recognize the number which the automated voice gave her.

Ruth wondered if Clare was in the pub with Steve or Sam. It was late, but if she hurried, she could make last orders. They were never in a hurry to throw you out. But then Ruth thought about the phone call. If you were going to burgle somewhere, what did you do? You rang up first to make sure that nobody was in. Ruth went round house, turning on lights. Then she made herself a mug of cocoa and put *Newsnight* on the TV.

"Britain has the worst burglary rate in Europe, but the police announced today that they will no longer automatically attend houses whose burglar alarms go off, because nine out of ten calls are false alarms. Meanwhile, new Home Office statistics say that half of all burglaries and thefts from cars are committed to fund drug habits," the presenter said, with his smug, head boy smile. "Later, we ask the Home Secretary what can be done to stop this rising tide of what is – some statistics suggest – increasingly violent crime. But, first, we hear from a senior policeman who thinks that now is the time for all drugs to be decriminalized."

That's all I need, Ruth thought, as she sipped her cocoa – not only am I about to be burgled, but the person who does it will be a psychotic crackhead who'll kill me for fun. She changed channels and waited for Clare to come in.

The night shift was already up and running, but Jan stayed behind deliberately, typing a report. Kevin was on call and Henry was still at Dawn's. Jan would pick him up on the way home. Only one more day, then she had a long weekend – not starting work on Sunday until ten at night. The only drag was that she and Kevin were expected for Sunday dinner at her in-laws. The Hunts still didn't think that Jan ought to be working, especially not at night.

Inspector Paul Grace seemed to share their attitude. He gave her a look which seemed to say "Still here?" as he walked through the parade room at twenty past ten. He looked tired. Jan didn't feel sympathetic. The way she saw it, senior officers were meant to arrive early and leave late, but they shouldn't expect everyone else to.

"Got a moment, sir?" she asked.

"Of course."

Grace parked his backside on the table.

"I wondered if you'd got anywhere with a replacement for Neil."

"I'm trying to find a transfer," Grace said, defensively, "but numbers are tight everywhere."

"I'm aware of that, sir. What's wrong with another probationer?"

"We've already got two – that's what's wrong. Clare Coppola's only been here five minutes!"

"She's been here as long as you, sir," Jan pointed out. "And Ben Shipman's nearly completed his probationary period. I think he'd like to work as a mentor."

"I'll give it some thought," Grace said.

His standard brush–off. But at least she'd said something. Jan got ready to go.

When Ben got back to his flat, he thought about ringing Ruth again. He'd tried to call her from a phonebox in town when he got off duty, but there was no reply. She'd probably gone for a drink with one of her many friends. And if she hadn't, if she'd just got in, it was too late now to suggest that they meet somewhere. Ben needed to talk to Ruth, but the phone in her house wasn't private enough for the kind of conversation he wanted to have.

The red light on his answering machine was flashing. Ben hoped it would be Ruth. It was Charlene.

"Hello, lover. If you're not back too late, give me a call. I miss you. Bye."

Ben didn't call Charlene. He'd not seen her since Sunday and it was now Wednesday. Charlene would want to know why. But Ben needed not to see her for a few days to allow him to think clearly, to work out what he wanted. It didn't help that his head was constantly heavy and he had a snuffle. He must have a cold coming on.

It seemed, lately, that all of his conversations with Charlene had an edge to them. Whereas, with Ruth, he could talk for hours about nothing in particular. They could drift from serious subjects to silly ones to silence. Charly treated silence like it was some kind of physical threat.

Ben missed Ruth. These last few days, he'd felt adrift. It wasn't just Ruth. He missed Neil, too. It was OK, working with Jan again, but the sergeant seemed to have a lot on her mind. They talked little, and the days dragged. Ben hoped for a new partner, one who he could strike up a rapport with.

Trouble was, Ben knew what was likely to happen. In a few weeks, he'd have passed his probationary period. Chances were that the sarge would put him with Clare Coppola. Jan was meant to be tutoring Clare, but the pair of them were like chalk and cheese. They pretended to get on, but were always on the verge of falling out. Ben got on with Clare all right socially. But, as an officer, he found her too wilful, too pushy. It didn't help that she was Ruth's best friend, either – although that was unfair, because if it wasn't for Clare, he would never have met Ruth.

Ruth. His thoughts kept coming back to her.

Unable to talk, Ben tried to put his feelings down in a letter. He got out a notepad, and wrote for an hour. The writing felt good. It felt – what was the word? – cathartic: as if he was being really honest for the first time. But when he read over what he'd written, it didn't come out as well as he wanted, so he wrote it again, adding more details, expressing his feelings more clearly.

By the time he'd finished, it was after two in the morning. Ben blew the ink dry and looked for an envelope. He meant to walk over to Ruth's now, before he slept, and put the letter through her door. He couldn't find an envelope anywhere. Ben never wrote letters these days. Practically all the letters he sent were bill payments, in ready-addressed envelopes. He would buy some in the morning. Ben went to bed, and slept soundly.

In the cool of the morning, Ben's cold was worse, but the high emotions of the night before had passed. Ben picked up the letter, all three A4 sides of it, meaning to go down to the sub-post-office on Mansfield Road, buy some envelopes, and post it. But then he reread part of the letter. His words embarrassed him. He had to skip parts because they were too candid. There were things here that he'd never shared with anyone. There were details about his relationship with Charlene which he'd never admitted to himself, never mind Charlene. Could he really have been within minutes of posting this the night before?

What would Ruth think if she got a letter like this? She kept insisting, after all, that their relationship was casual. "No strings," she was fond of saying. But they were past that now. There might be no strings, but she'd made it clear she wouldn't tolerate his cheating on her. What woman would?

Was Ben's relationship with Ruth wishful thinking? Maybe there was nothing there at all. It wasn't Ruth he was looking for, but a reason to break up with Charly. Maybe Ben knew, deep down, that he had come to the end of the line with Charlene, so had chosen someone who was the exact opposite of his girlfriend.

Charly was glamorous, exciting and intellectual. These were the qualities which had first drawn him to her, in their second term at university. She was vain back then, too, and calculating, and incredibly ambitious. But she also had an infectious idealism which now seemed like naïvety. It had long since been replaced by a rigid formula of political correctness.

Ruth on the other hand... Ben didn't know any more. He didn't know anything.

Ben picked up the letter he'd struggled so long over, screwed it up in a ball in his hand, and threw it into the bin. He drank a pint of orange juice, hoping that the vitamin C would help ward off his cold. He would go for a run before breakfast. Ben changed into his tracksuit, glancing at the bin as he hurried out. All that he could see of the letter was the last line, three small words that he'd never said to Ruth, not yet, anyway.

I love you

Closing the door behind him, he began to run.

14

Thursday came and Thursday went. During the day, Clare finished her share of the interviews at Greencoat. Everyone who had anything to say, and many who didn't, had been interviewed. Clare did fifty-three interviews in all, and learnt nothing of value from any of them. For two nights, she'd kept her pager by the bedside, expecting a call. It didn't come. If Phoenix had ignited a fifth target, neither the Fire Brigade nor the media had been informed. Chris Dylan's theory of a fire every four days was beginning to look dubious.

Clare stayed up late both nights, watching the Tableworks videos and talking to Ruth. Ruth's relationship with Ben had reached crisis point.

Clare was glad that Neil wasn't around. If he was, the two of them would have ended up acting as go-betweens for Ruth and Ben. But they had their own relationship to sort out. Clare had avoided seeing Steve since their drink together. But she was always aware of him there, waiting in the wings: attractive, intelligent, and dangerous.

After four late afternoons and nights watching, Clare had somehow got through twenty-four hours of videotape. It was tempting to fast forward and picture search, particularly on the early weekday mornings when there were hardly any customers. But Phoenix kept odd hours. You couldn't second-guess when the arsonist might enter the shop. In the meantime, Clare felt like she was watching a silent movie with no plot. She even saw the shop in her dreams at night.

Clare was probably carrying out a wild goose chase. But she wanted to show Dylan that she had a capacity for thorough, methodical work, even if it killed her. The detective sergeant hadn't yet said whether he'd need her the following week.

Impatient for action, Clare went into the CID offices on Friday morning. DS Dylan wasn't in the incident room. DI Greasby was.

"Clare, isn't it?" he said. "I hope you know that aides to CID always make the tea."

"I'm supposed to be off duty," Clare said, not sure if, technically, she was or not.

"Then what are you doing here?"

Clare smiled.

"Who wants tea?" she asked.

It was interesting to observe the incident room. Six officers were assigned to what had become "Operation Phoenix". Dylan was investigating the school fire. Greasby and another DS were looking at the factory fire and the earlier night club fire. Two DCs were investigating the attacks on the bank and the library. They were both in the incident room, writing up their case notes. One of them, Tracey, had interviewed Clare about the library attack. Clare brought her a mug of tea.

"Any luck?"

Tracey sipped her tea, then added Sweet 'n' Low to it.

"Not really. Until the letter from Phoenix arrived, we spent all our time looking for people who had a grudge against the places attacked. Lots of people have it in for banks, for instance. Then there are people who've been sacked at the factory, and so on. But ... a library? Who'd have a motive to burn down a library? Someone fed up because they got a fine on an overdue book?"

Clare laughed.

"So you're taking this serial arsonist business seriously?"

"It's the only thing that makes sense. Some kid, perhaps, after publicity."

"Then why didn't they claim credit after the first or second attack?"

Tracey considered Clare's question.

"Maybe it took the first four for them to build up the confidence to boast about it. After one or two fires, we might not take them seriously. But after five…"

"In that case, why wasn't there a fire yesterday?"

Greasby turned round from the noticeboard.

"Maybe there was."

"What do you mean?" Clare asked him.

"Somebody burnt down a derelict house near the Arboretum. Same MO. Petrol seems to have been used. No threat to people. Only thing is, the media didn't receive a letter this time. Possibly been delayed in the post. Wait and see time."

"No one called me," Clare complained.

Greasby gave her a funny look.

"Anyone ever told you that you've got a big head?" Tracey asked, as the detective inspector took a phone call.

DS Dylan breezed into the room.

"No rubber-stamped confessions in the second post," he announced. "Hello, Clare. Isn't it your rest day?"

"I thought I'd see what's going on," she said.

"And have you?"

"I guess…"

Dylan sat down.

"Anyway, thanks for your help at Greencoat School. It was appreciated. I'll make sure that a note goes in your file."

"We didn't get anywhere, though, did we?"

"You never know," Dylan grinned. "I checked the register. Scott James had an unauthorized absence on the day before the bank attack. Interesting, eh?"

"Maybe."

"Unfortunately, he's got a paper round, which seems to act as an alibi for the factory fire, but we'll interview him again."

"Do you want me to…"

Dylan shook his head.

"You've done your bit. Enjoy your rest days."

"I'm perfectly willing to stay and help today," Clare insisted. Earlier in the week, he'd seemed so keen for her to help.

"I'm sure you are," Dylan said. "But there's nothing for you to do. Anyway – truth is, I've got a trainee detective constable starting on Tuesday. I can't really supervise an aide as well."

"Neil."

"Neil Foster, yes. Of course. He was in your shift, wasn't he?"

Only when she was out of the door did she remember the videotapes. Dylan had clearly forgotten them. So he couldn't stop her looking, could he?

*   *   *

Charlene was angry. She'd hoped to spend the whole weekend with Ben, at least until he started night shift on Sunday. Then she would drive to see her parents in London on Easter Monday. Instead he'd left a message on her machine. It said he was going away for a couple of days "to think". Whatever he had to *think* about, she hoped he got it out of his system.

What was it with Ben? She had accepted him joining the police, though she didn't like it. She'd moved to Nottingham to be near him. She knew that he'd been seeing a bit of another woman, a mousy policewoman called Ruth. He'd said she was just a friend, and Charlene didn't ask if the relationship was sexual. She didn't want to know. In London, she'd been out with other men, Ben knew that. But she hadn't slept with any of them. She'd never been with any man but Ben, never wanted to. However, the way Charlene saw it, they'd been together since they were nineteen. Maybe they ought to see other people before they settled down, got married, had kids. She didn't want Ben to feel trapped.

For as long as Charlene could remember, her life had been work, work, work and work. When did she get to play in the sunshine? Why was it that, when her phone rang, she found herself praying it would be Ben, and he'd have changed his mind?

"Ms Harris?" a plummy voice said. "It's Roger

Wellington here. We met at Ian's house on Saturday."

Charlene was confused. Why was the MP calling her rather than her boss?

"Of course, yes. Hello, Mr Wellington."

"Roger."

"And I'm Charlene. What can I do for you?"

"The thing is, I've just moved into this apartment, and I believe we're neighbours."

"So Mr … Ian told me."

"Now I know this is short notice, but I'm giving a little dinner on Monday night and I wondered if you'd be able to join me."

Charlene took a deep breath and calculated. She could go to Mum and Dad's tomorrow, instead of Monday, then come back in time for the dinner. It was a good thing Wellington wasn't asking Ben, too. After all, she could hardly refuse, but Ben wouldn't be seen dead at the ex-minister's flat.

"Do say if it's inconvenient," Wellington told her. "I realize it's Easter and all that, but I thought, with you being new in the city…"

"I'd be delighted," Charlene said.

Clare was up to Thursday afternoon. The videos had become a kind of standing joke in the house. No one else could get near the TV. Ruth had brought her portable down into the kitchen so that Sam could keep up with *Brookside*. When the phone rang, interrupting her viewing, Clare expected it to be Neil. He would want her to go out tonight, even though they were going to a party tomorrow and having Easter dinner with his mum on Sunday.

But it wasn't Neil. It was Ben. His voice sounded unusually gruff.

"How's life with CID?" he asked.

"Bit of an anti–climax. I'm back with the shift on Sunday night. Have I missed anything?"

"Nah. It's been really quiet. Good thing, as we still haven't got a replacement for Neil. Look, is Ruth there?"

"I'll check."

Clare went to the kitchen and spoke before looking.

"Ruth?"

Two irritated faces looked up. She had interrupted Sam and Steve in some kind of deep conversation. Clare apologized.

"I think she went out," Steve said.

Clare checked Ruth's room, but she wasn't there.

"Can I take a message?" she asked Ben. "Shall I get her to call you back?"

"No." Ben's voice was uncharacteristically hesitant. "Tell her … I have to go away for the weekend. Tell her … that I'm thinking about her. Got that? She'll know what I mean."

"I've got that," Clare said.

Ruth came back an hour later. She'd been for a walk, as she often did these days.

"Did you go past Ben's?" Clare asked.

"I did. He was in, but her car wasn't there. How did you guess?"

Clare told her.

Phoenix bought a paper on Friday evening. There was an article on page five about a house being burnt down. A DI Greasby said that police "hadn't ruled out the possibility that it was the work of the serial arsonist who describes himself as 'Phoenix'." The police were really stupid. Phoenix had always known that. They expected another fire, regular as clockwork. But some fires took longer to prepare than others.

Phoenix typed out the letter. This was Easter weekend. There was no delivery until Tuesday. If the letter went in the post on Saturday morning, it should arrive by first post on Tuesday. Therefore, to obtain maximum impact, the fire should be set late on Easter Monday, or even early on the Tuesday morning. The letter read as follows:

IVE DECIDED TO GO OUT WITH A BANG!

IF YOU DON'T CATCH ME THIS TIME THEN YOU NEVER WILL

GOOD LUCK. YOU'LL NEED IT.

PS THE HOUSE FIRE WASNT ME. WHAT DO YOU THINK I AM – SMALL FRY?

15

Ruth had Easter Monday off. Ben was on nights, which meant that, if she was to see him this week, it would have to be this afternoon. But he hadn't called again, and Clare said he'd been off sick the night before. Ruth rang Ben's flat, but only got the answering machine. She hung up the phone without leaving a message. Probably he was with his family in Mansfield. Ruth didn't feel that she could call him there.

It was late afternoon. Sam and Steve were out, and Clare was asleep upstairs. There was a banging on the front door. Ruth put the chain on and answered it.

"Hilda!" She recognized her next-door neighbour. "What's wrong?"

"Someone's been in my house again!"

Ruth took the chain off hurriedly.

"You'd better come in."

She ushered the old lady into the untidy living-room.

"Have you called the police?" she asked.

"No point, is there?"

Hilda sat down.

"Now, come on," Ruth said. "I know that they didn't do much last time, but a burglary's a burglary, isn't it?"

Hilda shook her head.

"What do you mean?" Ruth asked. "What did they take?"

"They didn't take anything," Hilda told her. "They put things back!"

Neil was glad to be back at work. He'd been looking forward to Easter, but it hadn't been a success. His mum started getting all tearful about him moving out and Clare wanted to spend all her time watching stupid store security videos. He'd practically had to drag her out to Sunday dinner because, she complained, there was one tape that she still hadn't watched. Clare also insisted on bringing Ruth to the party on Saturday night, even though Ruth was currently as much fun as a wet weekend. The two girls had gone home together, early. Neil got drunk to compensate, so that, on

Sunday, he was hung-over and bad-tempered.

But now he was at work for CID. There was only a skeleton staff on today – blokes without families, mostly. Neil was keen to show up because he was having the next day off to move house. He and DS Dylan were going to visit the home of a fifteen-year-old youth called Scott James on Leybrook Close, a small cul-de-sac in Aspley.

"He's still in bed," Mrs James told them.

"At four in the afternoon?"

"These are the school holidays, you know."

They waited in the kitchen. The house was one of a number of three-bedroom council houses set behind Greencoat School. They were fairly modern and, Neil knew, coveted by tenants seeking transfers. But he wouldn't like to live in one himself. The outsides all looked the same: a collection of oblongs built out of sandy red brick with PVC windows. Inside, they had a plastic, pretend feeling, as though they weren't real homes, but some distant architect's idea of what a real home was.

There was some shouting upstairs. Seconds later, Scott James came down, wearing only underpants. He was pulling an "I love Hate and I hate everything else!" T-shirt over his skinny, hairless chest.

"What do you want?" He slurred his words. "Already told you I don't know nothing."

"You haven't told my colleague and I anything," Dylan said, in a cold voice. "And we're going to disregard any lies you've told in the past, just as long as you tell us the truth now."

Dylan nodded at Neil. This was the bit that Neil had been dreading. A real live interview with a serious suspect, being assessed by his tutor officer. This was his chance to blow it, big time.

"Where were you on Friday night, three weeks ago?" Neil asked.

"How the hell should I know? That wasn't when the school burnt down."

"I'm not asking you about the school," Neil said. "So think back carefully. Where do you usually spend Fridays?"

"Depends, doesn't it?"

James was waking up now. An irritating, boastful grin began to spread across his face.

"Depends on what?" Neil asked.

"On whether I've been able to score."

Ben must be back, Charlene knew that. He'd started on nights the day before. But he hadn't called her and Charlene was getting nervous. She didn't understand. What had she done wrong?

But there was no time to think about that now. For tonight's dinner party, she chose a more elegant dress than the one she'd worn the week before – a red silk number with straps so sheer that a piece of paper could cut them. She wondered who else would be there, hoping that the conversation wouldn't all be politics. Not that Charlene minded arguing with people she didn't agree with. In fact, she liked a good argument.

Roger "Welly" Wellington didn't intimidate her. Charlene had been the best performer at her school's debating society. That was one thing which had persuaded to go into the law. Back then, she'd meant to be a barrister, before she realized how much money you needed behind you to get started.

But Charlene liked to talk about things other than politics. Culture, mainly. She was hungry to learn about opera, plays and poetry. There'd been a time when she and Ben explored new stuff all the time. But not lately.

Wellington's apartment was higher up the hill than Charlene's tiny studio flat. She'd bet he had an excellent view. The MP opened the door himself. Surprisingly, he was wearing an open-necked shirt. Wellington took Charlene's coat, and complimented her dress extravagantly. Charlene praised the apartment, though all she could see was the wide hallway, furnished with original paintings which were surprisingly modern.

"I hope you'll feel at home here," Wellington said.

"It's certainly big," Charlene found herself burbling, out of her depth for a moment. "You could fit my place into this hall. But you live here alone?" Why had she said that? Jagger had already told her that he did.

"I have a daughter," Wellington said, "Emma. I've given her a key and asked her to treat the place as a second home. My wife and I are ... separated. Emma blames me for the breakdown of the marriage. I hope that, now I've returned to Nottingham, I'll be able to make things up with her."

"I hope so," Charlene said, surprised by the MP's candour.

She glanced into the living-room. The table was candlelit. Soft music played, but she couldn't hear any conversation.

"Champagne?"

Wellington had brought an ice bucket from the kitchen.

"That'd be lovely."

"This way."

Charlene followed Roger Wellington into the living-room and looked all around.

"Where is everybody?" she asked.

"Finish your videos?" Jan enquired, when Clare joined her in the parade room at five to ten.

"I'm half-way through the last one," Clare said. "Two hours to go. I'd have seen more, but a funny thing happened."

"What?"

"I told you about the burglaries on our street — three so far."

"Yes."

"Well, the little old lady next door got broken into again — only they didn't take anything this time, they put things back."

"You're kidding!"

"No," Clare insisted. "Her radio and VCR were exactly where they'd been originally. Only the remote control for the video was missing. No prints. No sign of forced entry, either. It's a mystery."

The phone rang. Jan picked it up, listened, said "I see" a couple of times, then, "Take care, bye."

"That was Ben," she told Clare. "He's off sick again. Flu."

"Good thing it's quiet," Clare observed.

Today was a bank holiday, more like a Sunday than a weekday.

"I had a call from CID," Jan said. "They want us to keep an eye on some lad — Scott James — DS Dylan said that you knew the score with him."

Clare explained.

"We'll drive by there first," Jan decided.

It was a mild April night. The moon was nearly full and the sky was almost clear. Everything was quiet, but the pubs hadn't thrown out yet. On TV, the live football game had just finished and the current teen heartthrob group were bringing the Royal Variety Performance to a frenetic finish. Jan and Clare parked at the end of a cul-de-sac near the edge of the council estate. There were lights on in 16, Leybrook Close. Loud music drifted down from an upstairs bedroom.

"What kind of music do you call that?" Jan asked.

"Techno," Clare told her. "It only makes sense if you take the right drugs."

"You'd know all about that, would you?" Jan teased.

Clare smiled.

"Sounds like he's in."

"Unfortunately for the neighbours. Shall we go?"

"Hold on."

The music had stopped. The bedroom light went out. Jan turned off the engine. A couple of minutes later, a tall figure in an anorak darted out of the front door, across the road and down a narrow ginnel which led towards the school playing fields.

"Think he's going to have another go at burning down Greencoat?" Jan asked. Then she radioed in a description.

"We'd better head around there to be on the safe side," Clare suggested.

They cruised around the school, but there was no sign of any intruder. Nor was there any trace of Scott James. Clare and Jan drove around for a little longer, then stopped outside the Oak Tree, a pub on the edge of the estate with a reputation for violence. There was no need to go in. The presence of a police panda in the car park would be enough to make the landlord call, "Finish your drinks," on time. Hopefully, it would also deter any of the drinkers from making mayhem as they left.

"Maybe Scott went for a drink," Clare suggested.
"Let's hope so," Jan said.

The petrol station normally closed at midnight.
However, on Sundays, it shut at eleven, so Phoenix
got there early in case bank holidays turned out to
be the same. They did. The place was already dark.
Phoenix got out the petrol. There was more of it
this time. Instead of milk bottles, Phoenix had used
two litre containers.

The thing about petrol stations, Phoenix worked
out, was that they were designed to resist fire. The
petrol was underground. The odd spill on the
tarmac quickly evaporated. What burnt wasn't the
petrol itself, but the vapours from the petrol. It was
necessary, therefore, to find the safety valve from
the station and ignite that. To create a really big
bang, you needed some other material to catch fire,
building up the heat until the petrol below started
to expand and ... *voilà!*

Phoenix had taken a long time to choose this
target. The petrol station was right by a discount
warehouse which had traded all weekend. No refuse
had been removed, so there was a huge pile of
cardboard boxes and other packing materials to be
taken, with no security worth speaking of. Phoenix
had staked the place out for two nights. A one-man
patrol came by once an hour, just after the hour.
The garage had its own alarm system, so the guard

didn't check there. Phoenix had an hour to build the fire and would light it as soon as the guard was gone.

It took time. The petrol station was in a small industrial area only a mile or so from the city. No one should be able to see, but, nevertheless, it was always possible that someone would come by, a jogger perhaps, or someone walking a dog. Phoenix hurried. At five to twelve, the fire was ready. Phoenix waited for the guard to come.

He was early. The van swept round the car park, pausing outside the warehouse goods entrance. Then it was gone.

Phoenix checked the escape route before getting the fuel out of its hiding place. Soon, it was being splashed all over the place. Thoughtfully, the petrol station had provided a tap for motorists to wash oily hands. Phoenix used it. There was always a thin chance of being stopped on the way back. Phoenix didn't want to have hands or clothes smelling of petrol. Finally, Phoenix tossed a lit match on to the ground, then ran back.

Flames snaked along the tarmac towards a pile of debris soaked in petrol. Within moments, it was all alight. A big flame appeared above the safety valve pipe. It was like something you only saw on television, broadcast from far away countries, or at sea. Phoenix smiled at the beauty of it all, then ran further back, to safety. Any moment now, all hell would break loose. Phoenix could hardly wait.

16

This was turning into another boring night. Clare shouldn't complain, but the thing was, the less action they saw, the longer the night seemed. It was always a struggle, adjusting to nights, and tonight she felt tired, her thoughts blurred.

"Is that who I think it is?" Jan asked, pointing across the road.

Clare slowed down. It was Scott James, in the anorak he'd been wearing earlier, walking briskly in the direction of home.

"I wonder where he's been," Clare said.

Jan wrote something down in her notebook. Clare drove back on to the ring road. There was a spectacular sunset over the allotments, she saw. Then she realized that you didn't get sunsets at midnight.

"Look!"

Jan radioed it in as Clare accelerated back the way they'd just come, towards the fire, siren on all the way. She couldn't tell if the fire was getting stronger or it was just that they were getting nearer.

"Which road do you reckon?" Clare asked Jan as they left their beat.

"Try the next right."

Clare skidded up a hill, around a church and down into a small valley. The fire was right in front of them. A factory, or some kind of warehouse, was alight on one side. Next to it was another structure, flames coiling around it like the breath of dragons. Behind it was a giant roman candle. Clare stared at the firework display with stunned fascination.

"What is that place?" she asked Jan, as they hurtled down the hill.

"Don't get any closer!" Jan stuttered. "I think it's a petrol station!"

Clare pulled the handbrake on. The car skidded to a stop as fire engines appeared on the road behind them. Clare did a knife-edge turn, the way she'd seen joy riders do, hoping that the firefighters would realize what was going on and not drive straight into them.

Then, as Clare tried to straighten the car up, half on the pavement, half on the road, the whole world exploded. The bang was so loud that it deafened both of them. They were surrounded by oranges and reds and bits of black, which smashed into the car. This wasn't real. It was something from a Hollywood special effects department. By the time the windows shattered, Clare was past caring. The heat was so intense, the flames so bright, she was sure that they were already dead.

Charlene sat on the sofa with Roger Wellington a few inches away from her. So far, as least, he'd behaved himself. That is, unless you counted his implying that she was one of many guests at a dinner party when, in reality, it was a candlelit dinner for two, with Charlene as the main course.

At least he could cook – or his caterers could – she wouldn't put that pretence above him. The food was exquisite, the wine excellent. The conversation was less interesting. Like most politicians, Wellington was an egotist. He enjoyed talking about himself. At first, Charlene flattered him by asking plenty of questions and laughing at his indiscreet anecdotes about colleagues. She would enjoy telling some of the better ones to Ben, later.

But, after a while, it got boring. Wellington made a show of being curious about her, but Charlene noticed how his eyes glazed over if she talked for more than a minute or two. She tried to change the conversation to more cultural subjects, but the ex-minister knew less about the arts than she did. His family was a no-go area. Charlene had heard enough "my wife doesn't understand me" stories from married middle-aged lawyers in London to last her several lifetimes.

Still, she had survived the evening so far. Now they were both on the sofa, with some Chopin in the background – a rather superficial choice, Charlene thought – and Roger had poured her twice as much Rémy Martin as she could possibly drink. Soon, he would make a move, which Charlene would politely refuse. She wouldn't tell the MP that she didn't fancy fat white men twice her age (though she didn't). No, she would mention Ben, and what a nice time she'd had, but explain that she would never have accepted his invitation if she'd known it was to be dinner for two. She wouldn't have wanted to give him the wrong idea.

Yes, Charlene thought, that should do it. Actually, the more she saw of Roger Wellington, the more she disliked him. Despite his expensive cologne, he had a dank, disturbing body odour. Some women thought of power as an aphrodisiac. Charlene wasn't one of them.

"Penny for your thoughts," the ex-minister said, softly.

"They usually cost more than that."

"Yes," he said, leaning over towards her. "I can see that you're a woman of expensive tastes."

Here it comes, Charlene thought. She was about to

say something when he lunged. His whole body seemed to wrap itself around her. For a moment, Charlene could hardly breathe, never mind protest. He pressed his mouth against hers while his hand groped her chest. Charlene managed to move her head clear.

"No," she said, firmly. "Stop."

But he didn't stop. Charlene thought for a moment that he was going to try and use force. How drunk was he? Then she heard something.

"There's someone coming in," she said.

That got his attention.

"What?"

"I heard someone…"

Wellington pulled away. Charlene realized that one of the straps of her dress had broken, so that the right side was hanging open. She was pulling it up when she saw a slim girl standing in the doorway, eyes blazing. The look on her face was one of disgust and disbelief.

"Hello, Dad," she said.

The sky was dark with debris, charred fragments from the fire which floated for a while, then fell like poison rain. An ambulance came and took Jan away. She was suffering from cuts and shock. Clare insisted on remaining.

"I didn't have time to register shock," she told DI Greasby, who had just arrived. "I was too busy driving, then braking, then ducking. I didn't see as much of it as Jan did."

The fire still raged. The fire brigade could do little beyond contain it with foam until the petrol had burnt itself out.

"Whoever did this," the Assistant Divisional Officer told Greasby, "was either very lucky, or knew precisely what they were doing."

Greasby brushed a bit of glass from Clare's hair which the medics had missed earlier. Acrid smoke filled Clare's lungs and she began to cough.

"Come on," Greasby said. "Whoever did this is long gone. Let's get you out of here."

"But that's why I had to stay," Clare said. "I think we saw who did it."

"You *what*?"

Minutes later, they were in the car, making the short journey to Leybrook Close.

"You're sure it was him?" Greasby asked for the second time. He was trying to stay calm, but his voice showed the excitement of a man who was about to make a major arrest.

"We saw him leave the house at ten twenty-five. We saw him walking back just after midnight. Jan made a note of the precise time."

"Was he carrying anything?"

"No."

Clare thought for a moment. "He didn't have the bag which I saw at the library. But the Fire Chief said that he'd have needed a lot more fuel than for the other fires. Maybe he'd hidden it there earlier."

"Good point."

"Next left. It's a cul-de-sac."

Greasby blocked the road.

"There's a little alleyway just over there."

"We'll wait a moment for back-up."

Clare pointed out Scott James's bedroom. Its light was off.

"He's probably at the back of the house, watching the fire," Greasby commented. Even here, half a mile away, the sky was lit like bonfire night.

Back-up arrived. One officer covered the alleyway, while another stood near the back of the house, ready to cover the back door the second Greasby knocked on the front one. Clare stood behind the detective inspector, hoping that James had come straight home, that he hadn't had time to destroy all evidence of his involvement in the fire.

Greasby rang the doorbell twice, then rapped on the door. It was a hard, official knock. The whole close could hear it, but Greasby added "Police!" for good measure. There was a clambering sound. Someone came downstairs. The door opened. It wasn't Scott. It was his mum.

"Detective Inspector Greasby, CID. Can I come in, please? It's urgent I speak to your son."

"At this time? It's after one! You've already seen him once today."

"I must insist."

Mrs James stood aside. She was wearing an old sports jacket instead of a dressing-gown. There was a gold chain with a crucifix on it around her pale neck.

"What's he done this time? I can't control him since his dad left. But he's not a bad lad, you know. He's not…"

Greasby was running up the stairs with Clare behind him. It was easy to identify Scott's bedroom. A sign on the door showed a smiley symbol smoking a joint. Greasby opened it without knocking. Clare stayed on the landing, in case Scott was in one of the other rooms and tried to escape. But he wasn't. Clare watched as Greasby announced:

"Scott James? We're police. You do not have to say anything, but…"

"Get her out of here!" Scott said in a whining voice.

He was naked, scrambling for a pair of underpants. Clare didn't look at the embarrassed boy, but at the contents of his room. The usual pop posters. A pile of comic books. A wet towel was scrunched up on the floor. She pointed it out to Greasby.

"Did you have a shower when you got in?" she asked the boy. He nodded.

"Where are the clothes you were wearing earlier?" Greasby asked.

"These are them," he said.

"Take them off again. We'll need them for the lab."

"What's all this about?" Mrs James asked.

"We'll explain at the station," Clare said. "Could you get him some fresh clothes, please?"

"I can't come to the station. I've got two young 'uns in bed."

"Clare. Go to the car," Greasby said. "Get some evidence bags, would you?"

Clare left. Outside, two uniforms dawdled by the front gate.

"Got him, did you?"

Clare smiled.

"Looks like it."

Suddenly, she felt very tired. She pointed at the Sierra.

"Please get the inspector some evidence bags. I think I'm going to faint."

One of them caught her, just in time.

"We'll be able to discharge you soon," the nurse told Jan. "Will your husband collect you?"

"No," Jan said. "He has to look after our child. I'll get a taxi."

"I'm sure we can sort out an ambulance or police car…"

"Could I have a mirror?" Jan asked the nurse.

"Sure. But you're not a pretty sight."

As the young woman walked away, Jan looked

around her. She was used to being in hospitals. Her husband worked in one. Many times she'd had to visit Casualty to check out possible criminal injuries. But the only time she'd been in as a patient was to have her baby, Henry. It felt odd, being here, behind the green screen, feeling like death warmed up. It felt terrible.

"Here."

Jan thanked the nurse and looked at her face in the mirror. Her black hair was singed and dusty-looking. Her face was covered with small cuts, several of which had needed stitching. Her chin was swollen and her cheeks were puffy. She didn't want anyone she knew to see her like this. The nurse returned.

"Handsome young man to see you."

Despite her earlier sentiment, Jan gave a sigh of relief. Kevin must have got someone to take Henry. Right now, she wanted to be cuddled, to be taken home and held tight all night.

"Jan."

It wasn't Kevin. It was Inspector Grace. He held a small bunch of anaemic-looking flowers. God knew where he got them at this time of the morning. Some all-night garage, probably.

"How are you?"

"I'll live."

"Let me take you home."

"Thanks."

Grace supported Jan as he took her to his car. He was the last person she wanted to see at this time, but he was her boss, and she couldn't turn him away. The inspector told her that Clare had been sent home, but before that, she had helped make a collar which looked "promising".

"Scott James?"

"I think that was the name, yes. You've done a good night's work."

"Thank you, sir."

"I want you to take as much time off as you need."

Jan waited for him to mention the desk job again, but he didn't.

"It's only a few cuts, sir. We're short-staffed as it is, with Neil gone and Ben off. I'll be back tomorrow."

"No," Grace insisted. "Take at least another day off. I'll hold the fort. And I'll have you a replacement for Neil by next week, I promise."

"Thank you, sir."

"How's Henry?" the inspector asked.

"Well, thank you."

Her son had had a bit of a sniffle when Jan came to work but she wasn't going to give Grace the details. When they got to Wollaton, she directed the inspector to her street. All of the lights were out in the house.

"Thanks for the lift, sir."

Grace waited in his car until Jan was safely inside,

then drove off. Jan's face hurt. Her body was stiff and her head was spinning. Somehow, she managed to climb upstairs, partially undress, and get into bed. Neither Kevin nor Henry woke up. When he wasn't on call, Kevin slept like the dead. Jan wasn't meant to get to bed until six-thirty. She couldn't sleep yet, but she couldn't get up, either. She lay awake for the next two hours, wondering how her husband would feel when he woke up next to an extra from a horror movie, wondering if the inspector was right, and it was time for her to get a desk job.

17

Clare got into the CID office just before seven. "It's him all right," Dylan told her, his voice both excited and cynical, "but he's refusing to talk. We're waiting for someone from the Social Services Emergency Duty scheme."

Since Scott was under eighteen, there had to be an "appropriate adult" present during his questioning. Scott's mother was looking after her other children and couldn't be with him, so that meant Social Services. Clare waited. She should have come off duty an hour ago. However, after fainting, she'd been taken home and had slept for a few hours. Now she was wide awake and ready for anything.

"How can you be sure it's him?" Clare asked. "What's the evidence?"

"So far," Dylan told her, "it's all circumstantial. Forensic will be looking at his clothes today. But he was in the right place at the right time. He had a shower when he got home. He looks guilty as hell."

Greasby came into the room. The inspector had been up all night and looked haggard. He spoke to Dylan.

"Social Services have arrived. He's ready to talk. You and Clare go in. I'll watch."

Scott James looked scared. His cheeks were sallow and his eyes were drained of colour. He was painfully thin, Clare realized. Inside his loose sweatshirt, Scott's body twisted and jerked spasmodically, like a stick insect on speed.

"He looks ill," Clare whispered to Greasby from outside the interview room door.

"The custody sergeant didn't think there was a problem when we brought him in," Greasby insisted.

"He did boast about drug taking yesterday," Dylan said. "But I thought he was trying to wind us up. Anyway, he's been here hours. What can he have taken?"

Clare was concerned.

"He looks completely out of it."

She turned to Greasby.

"Has the police surgeon seen him?"

DI Greasby shook his head.

"I'll be monitoring the interview from outside. If it looks like you're right, I'll send for him."

Dylan and Clare went into the interview room. Dylan took out the sealed taped bag and put two cassette tapes into the recorder. When the red light came on, he spoke.

"This is DS Dylan at seven ten a.m. on Tuesday the twenty-third of April. Interview with Scott James. Also present in the room are Mr Johal from Social Services and PC Coppola."

He confirmed that Scott had been properly cautioned. Then, before he could ask any questions, Scott said:

"I've got nothing to add to my earlier statement."

"You didn't tell us a lot in your earlier statement, Scott. We only want to know a few things. Where did you go last night?"

"No comment."

"Come on, Scott. Just tell me, for your own sake, who did you see?"

"No comment."

He sounded scared, Clare thought. Dylan kept pushing.

"All you have to do is answer those two questions, and we'll release you, no problem."

"No comment."

There was a long silence. Scott avoided eye contact, but, behind a blank stare, his eyes were glazed. He kept his hands beneath the table but Clare would bet that they were trembling. Dylan glanced at Clare. She spoke softly.

"What have you taken, Scott? Acid? E?"

His body seemed to buckle a little.

"No comment."

Clare tried to sound concerned.

"I know that something's wrong, Scott. We've met before, remember. You don't normally look like this. Do you feel well?"

"I don't feel great. That's 'cos you locked me up."

"You look dehydrated. Do you want a drink?"

"Yes, please."

"I'll get some tea," Dylan said.

"Not tea," Clare said. "Water. Lots of it."

A minute later, a bottle of mineral water arrived. Scott gulped at it thirstily.

"If you don't feel better soon," Clare told him, "we'll get you a doctor."

Scott kept drinking. Clare leant across the table to establish more intimate contact with him.

"Listen, Scott. We're not the drugs squad. We want to help you. Tell me, for your sake, what did you take?"

This time, Scott didn't glance at the Social Services man before replying.

"Bloke outside told me it was Ecstasy, but I don't think it was."

"Describe it to me."

"Brown. Round. It had little grey dots in it. I paid twenty quid."

"Have you ever taken Ecstasy before, Scott?

Would you know what to expect?"

Scott shook his head.

"I n-knew I'd been ripped off. The bloke at the door, he said, 'You didn't buy anything off him?' in this dead sarky tone. Then he laughed. Wouldn't let me into the rave. That's why I came home."

"Were you with friends?"

"What friends?" Scott replied in a bitter voice.

"Where was the rave?"

Scott still looked unsure.

"Come on, Scott," Dylan said. "This is your alibi."

"Think anyone'll admit to having seen me?"

He had a point, Clare realized. She asked another question.

"Are we talking about a warehouse party in Hyson Green, Scott?"

He nodded.

"Answer 'yes' for the tape recorder, please," Dylan said.

"Yes."

Clare calculated. It would take Scott forty-five minutes to an hour to walk to Hyson Green and the same amount of time to walk back again. The timing fitted precisely.

"Did anything else happen, Scott?" Dylan enquired. "On the way back, perhaps?"

"I went home, straight to bed. I thought I'd been ripped off. Then I started feeling crap – headaches, sweats – I had a shower, but I still couldn't get to sleep. Then you lot arrived and everything turned weird."

Dylan concluded the interview.

"Well," he said to Clare when they were outside, "that screws up our case."

"I believe him," Clare said. "Don't you?"

Dylan shrugged.

"He was convincing, all right. I don't know if he was telling the truth, though. We'll check the tablet he described with the drug squad as soon as someone's in."

"Will you get the police surgeon now?"

"I'll have to check with the boss. He may want to keep James in until the forensic report comes. If we're keeping him, we'll get the surgeon. If not, he's probably better off going to his own doctor."

Greasby was in the incident room, holding a sheet of paper.

"We just got this from Radio Trent. The *Post* and Radio Nottingham got one too."

"Phoenix claiming responsibility?" Clare asked.

Greasby nodded.

"That's not all he claims."

Clare read the letter.

"The last one?"

Dylan read it too.

"We'd better hope that Scott James is lying through his teeth," he said. "Otherwise, we're back where we started, with no worthwhile leads what-soever."

Phoenix had breakfast, then listened to the local news on the radio. Phoenix was the lead story on each station. No one had been hurt, unless you counted a policewoman treated for shock and minor cuts. The fire had been even more successful than Phoenix hoped. Phoenix had not only burnt down the petrol station, but the discount warehouse as well. It felt good. It felt like revenge.

Phoenix watched the lunchtime news on TV, waiting for the East Midlands section at the end. The final part of the story was news, even to Phoenix.

"Police confirm that they have been holding a suspect since shortly after the arson attack, but no charges have yet been made. I understand that CID are waiting for the results of forensic tests."

Phoenix cursed. The last thing Phoenix wanted was someone else claiming responsibility for the series of fires. Who had the police got? It was probably some headcase, someone who'd seen the explosion and wandered into a police station to take credit. The police would soon work out that, whoever it was, it wasn't Phoenix. There was only one Phoenix.

18

Charlene had to drag herself into work on Tuesday morning. The evening had been humiliating. Wellington's teenage daughter had watched as she extricated herself from the house, staring at Charlene's torn dress like she was a prostitute. Wellington had offered to call Charlene a taxi, forgetting that she only lived down the road. Charlene had grabbed her coat and left without responding. As she'd hurried out of the flat, Charlene had heard father and daughter yelling at each other. It was a very depressing night.

To make things worse, Wellington showed up at the office this morning five minutes after she did. The MP had bags under his eyes. Charlene thought he must have come to apologize, but he ignored her, and went straight to Jagger's room, where he stayed for two hours. Hearing him in the corridor, Charlene slipped to the toilet and stayed till he'd gone.

"Good holiday?" Ian Jagger asked Charlene an hour later, at lunchtime.

"So–so."

"You look a little under the weather."

A secretary left the room and they were in the office alone.

"It's nothing."

"I heard on the radio that they let the suspect in the Phoenix case go."

"Really?"

Snap out of it, Charlene told herself. *Make conversation.* But she couldn't.

"Has your boyfriend – Ben, isn't it? – has he been involved in the case?"

"I don't … I don't know."

Jagger leant over, his eyes full of concern.

"What's wrong?"

Charlene got up.

"Excuse me. I need the bathroom."

"Charlene, what is it?"

"It's nothing."

Jagger wrinkled his curly eyebrows, like a benevolent grandfather in a Disney movie.

"You said that a moment ago, and I didn't believe you then. What is it?"

Charlene tried to keep it together, but couldn't help herself. She burst into tears.

"There, there."

Jagger put an arm around her. He smelt of old-fashioned cologne.

"There, there."

Charlene found herself crying on his shoulder, her words sputtering out.

"I don't know where Ben is or who he's with. I heard he's ill but I don't know if it's true. I think he's split up with me, but he hasn't said so. I don't know anything."

"There, there."

Jagger handed her a clean cotton handkerchief from his breast pocket. Charlene wiped her eyes.

"Maybe you ought to take the day off," he said.

She shook her head.

"I've just had three days off and I hated every one of them. I want to work. It takes my mind off things. If you want to help me, give me more to do."

"Of course."

Jagger went to his office and returned with a fat bunch of files.

"You remember this man? Stormed out of my office last week swearing slander. His name's Adam Benson. He owes us nearly a thousand in fees, but he's about to go bankrupt. We're within our rights to hold on to all his files until he pays us, but he keeps ringing or calling round and making a nuisance of himself. I want rid of him. I'd like you to check that everything's in order. Remove any notes which aren't relevant, then return the lot to him."

"Fine."

"I know it's not that interesting. We'll find you something juicier soon, I promise."

"Thanks. And … thanks for just now, too."

"Any time," Jagger said. "Night or day. You know where to find me."

Her boss returned to his office. He was so nice to her, so genuine, that Charlene found it hard to believe any of the things Ben said about him.

Clare woke at five on Wednesday afternoon. The day before, she'd done a night shift, straight after helping CID during the day, and she was exhausted. CID hadn't got anywhere. There'd been a second letter from Phoenix, and forensic had confirmed that the typewriter used in the notes was an electric one: a Hermes 505, quite a common domestic machine fifteen years ago, and impossible to trace. That left the rubber stamp as a clue, though no one but her seemed very interested in it. Clare still hadn't had time to finish checking the Tableworks videos. More pressingly, she hadn't gone round to see Neil in his new house. He'd been expecting her yesterday evening.

Guiltily, Clare went to Ruth's room and took her car keys. She was on the insurance now, and Ruth let her use the car when she hadn't taken it to work herself. Clare popped over to ASDA, then drove to Suzie's Flower Shop in Sherwood, where she bought a big bunch of lilies. She cut through Watcombe Circus to Carrington, Neil's new home. As she got out of Ruth's car, Neil got out of his. He gave her a big smile. They kissed, then she handed him the flowers.

"Happy house-warming. I'm sorry I didn't come round yesterday."

"It's OK. The house was a mess. Chris Dylan told me how much help you'd been giving him. How's Jan?"

"OK, I think. She's back on tonight. Not sure about Ben. But last night, with them both off, was hell. We never stopped. They still haven't replaced you yet, which doesn't help."

"Let's not talk about work," Neil said. "Sometimes it seems like all we do is talk about work. Come inside. Let me show you my kingdom."

He unlocked the door. The house was smaller than Clare remembered, but it already felt homely. Clare put the lilies in water and a bottle in the fridge. She wanted to ask Neil what progress had been made on the Phoenix case today. Not a lot, from the way he'd spoken earlier. But he was right, they talked too much about work. Sometimes, it seemed that the police force was the only thing they had in common.

The house had three floors. The first contained a living-room and kitchen. The second had a bed-room and a bathroom. The third was an attic.

"Your study?" Clare asked, looking around the top room. It had a peculiar shape. The odd angles gave it character. From a high window you could see Neil's narrow patch of garden below.

"It *could* be a study," Neil said. "But what would I want a study for? I was thinking more of a spare bedroom."

He pointed to a corner.

"There's plenty of room for a built-in wardrobe there."

"Yes, there is," Clare agreed.

She was conscious that Neil was imagining her clothes, filling it. She was thinking of Steve, wondering if his attic room was like this. No, his would be bigger. She'd been working so much that she hadn't seen much of Steve recently, which was probably for the best.

"What's wrong with Ben?" Neil asked, when they were back downstairs, later, drinking the sparkling wine which Clare had bought at ASDA.

"Flu, I think. He's staying at his parents. Ruth's pretty frantic because she hasn't spoken to him for ten days."

"She knew what she was getting into," Neil said. "Ben's on the rebound from a five-year relationship. He's not going to rush into another commitment."

"It's not that," Clare said. "Ruth knows that he's still sleeping with Charlene."

"Ah."

Clare interpreted the look in Neil's eyes.

"You knew, didn't you?"

"Kind of."

"But you didn't tell me."

Neil nodded.

"Ruth's your best friend. Ben was my partner. Conflict of interest."

"I guess you're right," Clare said.

Her stomach began to grumble loudly, changing the subject.

"You're hungry," Neil said. "I'll order a take out."

"No," Clare told him. "I brought some groceries with me. It'll take me fifteen minutes to cook. I want to christen your new kitchen."

Neil's eyes lit up. He was easy to please.

"Great."

Clare made penne with broccoli and pine nuts. They drank the rest of the cava as they ate. As soon as they'd finished, Clare felt incredibly tired. She'd meant to go home and watch some more of the video before work, but she couldn't keep her eyes open. She and Neil sat on the mangy sofa which his mother had given him. She leant her head on his shoulder.

The next thing she knew, he was shaking her awake.

"Clare. It's half nine. You have to be at work soon."

"Uh … what?"

He'd put a blanket around her, she found. Clare's body was stiff. She needed a shower but there wasn't time for one.

"I'll drive you in."

"No. My uniform's at home and I have to return Ruth's car."

"All right," Neil said. "I'll follow you home. You can get changed, then I'll drive you in. Otherwise, you'll be late."

Clare agreed that this was a good idea. Neil was so thoughtful, she realized as she drove back to Forest Fields with him close behind. All he wanted was to be with her, to look after her. He asked so little in return. She'd be mad to let him go.

Ruth got home at half past ten. Her car wasn't where she'd left it and, for a moment, she thought it had been stolen. But it was a little way up the street. Clare must have been using it.

The house was dark. There was no one in. Nor were there any notes for her by the phone. With her next pay cheque, Ruth decided, she'd buy an answering machine, make sure she didn't miss any calls. But then it would be even more humiliating if she didn't get any.

Ruth was about to go upstairs when she heard a noise from upstairs: a shuffling, followed by a banging. She listened a moment more, then turned the light back out. Breathing deeply, she dialled three nines.

The call made, Ruth went into the kitchen. Then, using her police torch, she found the biggest knife in the drawer. The shuffling stopped. A door opened and closed. Standing in the hall, Ruth began to shiver. If he came downstairs now, in the dark, what chance did she have? The burglar was bound to be armed. They always were these days, even if all they carried was a sharp screwdriver. Ruth clenched the knife tightly.

There was another loud noise and Ruth was tempted to run outside. She didn't want to face whoever it was on her own. She tiptoed into the living-room and looked through the curtains. There were flashing blue lights in the street. Wisely, the officers attending the call had not turned their sirens on. Ruth crept back into the hall and opened the front door softly. To her surprise, the people getting out of the car were Clare and Ben.

Ruth managed half a smile for Ben. Her boy-friend – if he still was that – shot her a look of concern and relief. This wasn't in their patch, but they had recognized the address and come anyway. Behind them, another police car was coming down the street.

"Upstairs," Ruth whispered. "Someone moving about. A lot of banging and scraping."

"All right," Ben said.

He looked gaunt. His illness had been genuine, Ruth realized. He squeezed her arm as two more police officers came in: it was Bob and Ian, from Ruth's shift.

"There's a fire escape at the back needs covering," Ruth said.

"Let's go," Ben said.

Bob went out the back. Clare switched the lights on, then yelled, "Police! Give yourselves up."

Ruth, Clare, Ben and Ian charged up the stairs. They opened each of the doors on the first floor. There was no one there. With Ben at the front, they squashed their way up to Steve's attic room. The burglar would be down the fire escape by now, Ruth reckoned. She should have gone outside with Bob.

There was a light on in Steve's room. It had been dark when she got home. Ben kicked the door open. Steve sat on the bed, in his underpants, staring at them.

"What the..." A torrent of swear words flew from his mouth. Ruth had never felt so embarrassed in her life.

"The whole house was dark," she said slowly, when Steve had finished. "I heard someone moving things about. I'm sorry. I couldn't see how it could be anything but a burglary."

"Understandable mistake," Ian muttered, backing out of the room. "We'll be off."

Steve was pulling his jeans on.

"Brought the whole force along, did you?"

Ruth backed out of the room, following Ben down the stairs. But Clare held her ground. Ruth heard her friend asking Steve what happened, but didn't hear the reply.

Ruth and Ben went into her room. His radio was making noises but he ignored it.

"I feel such a fool," Ruth said.

He held her.

"Better safe than sorry," he told her.

"I've missed you," she said.

They kissed. His mouth tasted of medicine.

"Am I getting germs?" she asked, when they gently pulled apart.

"I'm over it now," Ben told her. "I had bad flu, a fever. I wanted to call, but my mum was nursing me. She was there all the time and..." Now he looked embarrassed.

"I didn't call Charly either. I needed time to think."

Ruth started to apologize.

"I should never have given you an ... an ultimatum like that. I kept saying that there were no strings ... I just lost my cool for a while. I'm sorry."

Ben shook his head.

"No. I'm the one who should be sorry. You were right. I had to choose."

He went quiet. Ruth whispered.

"And did you?"

There was a knock on the door and Clare came in.

"Steve was getting his guitar out of the loft," she explained. "That's what you heard."

"I didn't even know there was a loft," Ruth said.

"There's a bit of space between the attic and the roof. He keeps some of his old stuff up there. He'd been in bed, asleep. That's why the house seemed dark when Ruth came in. It was dark when I came home an hour ago, too."

Ruth was confused.

"He went up to the loft in his *underpants*?"

Clare became irritated.

"Maybe he got his clothes dusty when he went up there so he had to change when he came down. I didn't ask him, all right? You can go up and check if you want."

Ruth laughed awkwardly.

"No. It's fine. I've made enough of a fool of myself with him already. Perhaps you were too busy looking at his body to ask the tough questions."

Clare gave Ruth a playful punch in the stomach.

"Come on," she said to Ben. "There's a fight at the Five Feathers and they're calling for back-up."

"Give me half a minute," he told Clare. "I'll join you in the car."

"When can we meet?" he asked, when Clare had gone.

"I don't know," she said. "This week, I'm

sleeping when you're working and you're sleeping when I'm free."

"And you're working when I'm free. I've got a rest day Friday."

"I don't finish until Friday night."

"All right," Ben said. "We'll spend Saturday together. I'll have seen Charlene by then. I'll sort things out."

"Good."

They kissed and he left. Ruth didn't know whether Ben had made a decision yet. But if he was definitely going to finish with her, he would have told her by now. Wouldn't he?

19

On Wednesday morning, Charlene finished the Benson paperwork. She felt sorry for the guy. He'd had a good business going, but got into cash-flow difficulties when a couple of clients went bust. Jagger had done his best to keep him from going under, but finally, and rather cruelly, the bank had pulled the plug.

Something about the bank made her think. It was the Lace Market branch of the Midshires. Charlene remembered Ben saying something about it. Wasn't that the bank where…? She'd check with Ben. It would give her an excuse to call him.

"Finished?"

Charlene smiled at her boss.

"How do we send it round? Post? Courier? Or do we get him to collect?"

Jagger shook his head.

"I don't want him in this office again, unless it's to pay his bill. Get one of the secretaries to send it by guaranteed next day delivery."

"Fine."

Jagger paused.

"What is it?"

"Pardon?" Charlene said.

"There's something you were on the verge of saying. What is it?"

"Oh, it's just…"

Charlene hesitated. For the first time, she was aware that there was an ethical problem with what she was thinking of doing. Her first duty was to the firm. She ought to consult Ian before doing anything.

"This bloke, Adam Benson."

"Yes?"

"He more or less fits the description of the person who attacked the Midshires Bank, doesn't he?"

"I'm sorry," Jagger said. "I don't remember the description."

"Thin. Medium to tall in height. White."

"That could be an awful lot of people."

"But Benson has a grudge against the bank, a serious one. And he's unbalanced, anyone can see that."

"I take your point."

"What if he's the arsonist?"

Jagger stroked his chin, thinking. When he spoke, he sounded like an academic conducting a seminar.

"Please define more carefully the terms of the question you're asking."

Charlene took a deep breath.

"There's a serial arsonist attacking various institutions which, for some reason, he has a grudge against. We have knowledge of a strong suspect who the police seem to have missed. Do we have a duty…"

Jagger interrupted.

"Our first duty is to the client. And, anyway, this arsonist has attacked many places. Who's to say that he has a grudge against any of the others?"

"He might have," Charlene argued.

"The school?"

"Maybe he went there."

"The petrol station and discount warehouse?"

"I don't…" Charlene thought of something. "Hold on."

She got the papers out of the big brown envelope again and shrieked.

"The warehouse – they owe him money! Two months overdue. Now we've got a motive for two of them. Surely…"

Jagger shook his head.

"We're still bound by client/lawyer privilege."

"But he's not our client any more," Charlene protested. "He sacked us. We're giving him his files back."

Jagger was unconvinced.

"Nevertheless, we *were* his solicitors."

Charlene tried another tack.

"Suppose, next time, he kills someone?"

Jagger frowned.

"The arsonist called Phoenix claims to have retired."

"Oh, sure."

Jagger stroked his chin again.

"If there was a way of getting information to the police without it being clear that it came from this firm, then, possibly…"

Charlene saw what he was getting at.

"Of course," Jagger added, "I wouldn't want to know anything about it."

"Of course," Charlene said, taking the warehouse bill to the photocopier.

"I do enjoy our little chats," Jagger said, then began humming something operatic as he returned to his office.

Charlene looked at her watch. Ben was on nights. It was too early to call him yet. He would be fast asleep and what she had to say wasn't for his answering machine. She would go over there in her lunch hour.

Ruth was due on at two. Steve was still upstairs, banging about. How did men manage to be so noisy? Ruth was starting to worry that she'd be late for work. But then Steve finally left the house, carrying a big laundry bag, and got into Sam's car. He must be heading for the laundry on Noel St.

Ruth already had her uniform on and wondered if she was being paranoid. What happened last night was incredibly embarrassing. Sam made a quip about it before she went off to work at midday. Ruth had never felt so foolish. She had shown herself up in front of Ben and Clare, the two people whose opinion meant the most to her.

But what if Steve had something to hide? Ruth couldn't reconcile the noises she'd heard with someone getting a guitar out of the loft. There had to be more to it than that. She got to Steve's room. The door was locked, but it was the same kind of lock as the one in Ruth's room. She'd practised on hers earlier and, with the smallest amount of skill, was able to open it in seconds.

The room was as it had been the night before: messy and male. Clothes, books and magazines were piled on top of other piles. Every surface was covered except for one, the seat of Steve's chair. Nothing odd about that, Ruth thought. He needs something to sit on. But then she looked again at all the piles of clothes. Why hadn't he taken more of this stuff to the laundry?

She looked up at the cracked ceiling. There, in the corner, was the entrance to the roof space. There was no door, only a bit of board that you moved. Ruth looked again at the chair. She could see the imprints of foot marks on the seat. That was why nothing was piled on it. He'd been up in the roof – again, just now. Ruth had to go up there too.

She moved the chair underneath the opening, got her torch out, and stood on it. Ruth was several inches shorter than Steve. She wished she had a step ladder. Ruth could reach to move the bit of board aside, but it wasn't easy for her to lift herself up and look in. Ruth was never terribly good at gym during her school-days. This was like one of those exercises where you had to grab on to a bar and pull your head and shoulders up over it, only it was harder because she was trying to get into a narrow space. She pushed the torch inside the loft then yanked her body up. Up. Up. Up. Not quite.

Sweating, Ruth wished that she hadn't got her uniform on. It would get mucky inside and out. But she was already going to be late for work and didn't have time to get changed. The second time, she lifted herself enough to balance a shoulder inside the loft, which gave her some leverage. Nearly. Almost. Another big push. It hurt, but she was in.

The roof space was barely a metre high. Ruth banged her head as she reached around for her torch. When she found the torch and turned it on, she got a disappointing surprise. The loft was almost empty. There was a black plastic bin liner in one corner. Ruth investigated. It contained some remnants of carpet and a pair of filthy curtains. The early stages of a bird's nest were being constructed in another corner. Ruth shone the torch around, but that was all there was to be seen. She was about to go back down when her torch accidentally caught something else, glinting from beneath the beginnings of the bird's nest.

Ruth didn't move the nest. She wasn't meant to be up here, after all. But she did take a closer look. The bottom of the nest seemed to contain a video remote control. Ruth wouldn't mind betting that it belonged to Hilda next door.

Ruth was filthy now, so she decided to look beyond the bird's nest. She was expecting to get to a wall, but there wasn't one, only wooden rafters, which she crawled under. How big was this loft? Steve's room wasn't as large as this. Ruth was confused, until she came to a trapdoor, the same shape as the gap above Steve's room. Suddenly, the whole thing was crystal clear.

There was nothing separating the roofs of the terraced houses in this block. All Steve had to do was wait until someone was out, then he could sneak in without even appearing to leave his own room! That was why it was never clear how the burglar broke in. That was why it had taken Sam so long to get him to come down when Mrs Patel thought they were being burgled. He said it was because he was playing loud music. In fact, he was still in the roof!

But where was all the other stuff? Ruth worked out what Steve was doing last night – unloading the attic ready to take the stolen goods out to sell. Steve hadn't gone to the laundry. He'd probably gone to a second-hand shop, or a pawnbroker. That was why he'd borrowed Sam's car, rather than walking. He was getting rid of the evidence. Ruth wondered if the remote control would be enough for a conviction.

She put the torch away and lowered herself carefully back down into Steve's room. She was so intent on her climb down that she didn't hear feet on the stairs, or Steve's door opening. It was only as she replaced the bit of wood which went over the entrance to the attic that she realized there was someone else in the room with her. As Ruth turned round, a familiar voice asked:

"What the hell do you think you're doing in here?"

20

Ben was in the middle of a dream where Jan introduced him to his new partner. The guy turned out to be Carl Price, the pillock who'd been on temporary attachment to the shift earlier in the year. In this dream, Ben kept answering the telephone, but there was no one at the other end. He thought that Carl was winding him up. Then Ben woke. Hadn't he put the answering machine on? But it wasn't the phone. It was the doorbell. Someone was being awfully persistent.

Ben got to the door just after the bell stopped ringing. He nearly went back upstairs again, but he was almost awake now and whatever it was must be important. He opened the door and saw Charlene, getting back into her car. On seeing him, she gave a great big smile, slammed the door and hurried over.

Charly shut the door behind her and kissed him.

"Where've you been?" she asked.

"I was ill. I only started work again last night."

She looked at him tenderly.

"You've lost weight. I'm sorry I woke you up. I have some news for you. Something I found out at work. It's about the arsonist."

Ben was bewildered.

"Why didn't you dial three nines? Why come and see me?"

"It's tricky," Charlene said. "I wanted to talk it over with you first."

Ben became edgy. They'd only been together two minutes and already he had the feeling that he was being manipulated.

"Can't it wait until I'm awake?"

Charly smiled and stroked his hair.

"I'll tell you what, I'll make some breakfast while you have a shower. Then we can talk all about it."

This is Charlene all over, Ben thought as he turned the controls up to "hot": she comes in and takes over. But not for much longer.

Yet, as Ben dried himself off, his irritation at being woken gave way to curiosity: what could Charlene know about the arsonist? He could see that any information she got at work would be awkward to explain. He hoped that whatever she'd got implicated Jagger in some way. What if it led to

Phoenix? This wasn't Ben's case, but if he came up with a good lead, it would do him no end of good.

In the kitchen she'd put out orange juice, coffee and croissants, freshly bought from "Naughty but Nice", down the road. Her smile was so open and loving that it was impossible for Ben not to feel tender towards her. He slurped the orange juice and she poured coffee. As Ben was putting honey on his croissant, he asked her, "So what's the news that's so important you came over in your lunch hour to tell me?"

"It's Phoenix," Charlene said, calmly. "I've found out who he is."

Clare looked at Ruth like she'd gone off her head. She was in a dressing-gown, with a truncheon in her hand. Ruth was still standing on Steve's chair.

"You woke me up," Clare said.

"Sorry."

"You scared the life out of me. I nearly called the police, but then I remembered what happened last night and thought I'd better see for myself. What were you doing up there?"

"It's Steve," Ruth said. "He's the burglar."

Clare shook her head.

"That's silly."

Ruth moved the chair back to where she'd got it.

"I'll explain downstairs," she said. "Let's get out of here. I need to call a squad car."

"You'd better pick up a clothes brush on the way," Clare told her. "You're covered in muck."

In the kitchen, after calling the station, Ruth explained to Clare what she'd discovered in the loft.

"It might not be Steve," Clare said. "A clever burglar would stash the stuff in someone else's loft, not their own."

"Who said he's clever?" Ruth asked, as Clare left the room. "You think having a degree means he's smart? Grow up. He's a greedy little boy, that's all. Hey, where're you going?"

"To get dressed," Clare called down the stairs. "I'm coming with you."

"Thanks, partner." Neil put the phone down.

"Partner?" Chris Dylan asked, as they sat together in the CID room.

"My ex-partner, Ben Shipman," Neil explained. "He's had a tip-off from a reliable source. Phoenix is a bloke called Adam Benson."

Chris looked dubious.

"Does he fit the profile?"

The typical profile of a random arsonist was someone like Scott James: immature, early teens to mid-twenties – lonely, attention-seeking, a fantasist.

"Not quite," Neil said, "but he has a motive and a half. This bloke, Benson, he's got a definite grudge against at least two of the places attacked, the bank and the discount warehouse. One owed him money, the other refused to lend it. Ben reckons that he's been using this Phoenix, serial arsonist image to cover up what are actually a series of revenge fires."

Dylan still looked dubious.

"How did your mate get this information?"

Neil hesitated. He had a good idea where it must have come from, but didn't want to say.

"Reliable informant. That's all I know."

"Fair enough. I'll check it with the boss."

A couple of minutes later, Dylan was back.

"Your bloke's a possible. He was interviewed a few days after the bank attack. The bank supplied his name on a list of a hundred people they'd turned down for a loan. Benson claimed to have been at work and said that he'd found an alternative source of finance, so had no cause for a grudge against the bank."

"Did anyone check his story?" Neil asked.

"No. The interviewing officer found him convincing. He was at work. The business seemed to be running smoothly."

"According to Ben's source, he'll have to declare himself bankrupt any day now."

"All right," Dylan said. "Let's get over there."

At first Ruth's partner, Roy Tate, was dubious about bringing Clare along. Then Ruth pointed out that Clare knew all the second-hand shops and pawnshops on the patch adjoining theirs.

"How long's this Steve been gone?" Roy asked.

"Less than half an hour," Ruth told him.

"We'll have to hope that he didn't manage to sell the stuff at the first place he went to."

They drove from shop to shop. Sam's old mini wasn't outside any of them, but they looked in anyway. Clare was sure that Steve wasn't a professional criminal. For one thing, he was too short of money. For another, a professional would never have taken the risk of returning Hilda's video and radio. Not being a professional, Steve wouldn't know which shops were willing to act as "fences". He would have to pretend to own the stuff he was selling, and only flog one thing at each shop. It would take longer that way.

Roy radioed CID and got the serial numbers of the two CD players and three videos which were missing. There was also a ghetto blaster but the owner hadn't been able to give a detailed enough description of it. They quickly exhausted the shops in Hyson Green, Forest Fields and Radford. None of the people working in them had seen anyone of Steve's description. They crossed the city into Sneinton, feeling out of luck.

"Maybe he's tossed the lot into the Trent," Roy suggested.

"Let's hope not," Ruth said. "We haven't got enough to hold him otherwise."

Clare wasn't sure if she wanted to have enough evidence against Steve. Whatever happened, she realized, they would no longer be able to stay in the house they had just moved into. It was a mess.

The first shop they came to in Sneinton sold second-hand TVs and videos. The owner was friendly.

"Yeah, bloke answering that description was here twenty minutes ago. Sold me this video." He pointed at a Matsui front loader. Roy checked the serial number.

"Don't tell me it's bent?"

"I'm afraid so," Roy told him. "Any idea where he went next?"

"He was looking to sell a CD machine. I suggested Archie's up the road, or one of the Carlton places. He might have gone there."

They thanked the man for his help, gave him a receipt for the video, and hurried up the hill towards Carlton. Archie had indeed bought a CD player from Steve, and a video as well. He had paid nearly a hundred pounds and was pretty angry.

"If I'd guessed they were nicked I'd only have given him half as much," he complained, only partly joking.

The shop they found Sam's mini parked outside was just off Carlton Hill.

"I think you'd better let me go in and make the arrest," Roy said.

"Too late," Clare told him. Steve was coming out of the shop, a smile on his face, empty-handed.

"Looks like he's unloaded the lot," Ruth observed.

Roy pulled the panda to a halt in front of the mini, blocking it in as Steve reached for the keys. Steve looked up for the first time. Seeing Ruth, Roy and Clare, his face fell. He looked at the car, then glanced up the road. He was trying to decide whether to make a run for it. Roy got out of the car, handcuffs already open.

"Don't even think about it," Roy told Steve.

Ignoring Steve, Ruth went into the second-hand shop to recover the video, ghetto blaster and CD player. A moment later, Steve was sitting in the back of the panda, next to Clare. His face was flushed and angry.

"Aren't you going to ask me why I did it?" he asked Clare, bitterly.

She shook her head.

"I expect you stole for the same reason they all do. You thought you could get away with it."

Steve was silent.

"Give me Sam's keys," Clare said, quietly. "I'm off duty. I'll drive the car back for her."

"They're in this pocket," Steve said, sullenly.

Handcuffed, he couldn't get the keys out. Clare reached into his jeans, embarrassed to be having such intimate contact with him at a moment like this. As she took the keys, Steve gripped her hand, tightly. Roy was still outside the car. For a moment, Clare thought Steve was going to threaten or even hurt her.

"You know," Steve said, his voice almost tender, "if you weren't a policewoman, I could have gone for you in a big way."

He released her hand. *And if you weren't a thief...* Clare thought. But she got out of the car without replying.

21

Neil Foster and Chris Dylan sped across the city in an unmarked Sierra. Back at the station, DI Greasby was arranging an identity parade. Normally, ID parades took a long while to set up, but tall white males aged fifteen to thirty weren't in short supply. Two other members of the Phoenix team had gone to pick up Scott James. The youth had no decent alibi for any of the Phoenix attacks and was still a strong suspect. Neil and Chris were on their way to arrest Adam Benson, the man who Ben had identified as the probable arsonist.

Benson's office was in a group of small workshops off a main road in West Bridgford. The firm was called Benson's Battles.

"What do you think they make, with a name like that?" Neil asked.

"No idea," Dylan said, as they pulled in outside the prefabricated building. "Detergent? Cough sweets?"

The answer became apparent as soon as they got inside. Men in grey overalls were carrying out stacks of shrink-wrapped cardboard boxes with names like "The Seven Samurai" and "The Killing Fields". They were war games.

Adam Benson sat alone in a small office, a crumpled figure with his head in his hands, watching.

"What's going on?" Neil asked, sympathetically.

"The receivers," Benson said. "They're taking it all away. I'm bankrupt."

"I'm sorry to hear that," Dylan said, cautiously.

No matter how much misery this man was in, they were still going to arrest him. Benson sat there, oblivious. He had yet to ask them who they were or what they wanted.

"How did it happen?" Neil asked.

"If I could just have carried on until Christmas," Benson said. "I would have got the orders, I know I would. I export to Japan and America. You know how long it takes to get paid? This is quality stuff — for adults, not kids — I was getting the reviews, the publicity, it was all about to take off…"

"What went wrong?" Neil asked.

"Credit. All I needed was another fifty thousand worth of credit. By the new year, I'd have turned the corner. But would they give it to me? No." A tear trickled down his face.

"Is that why you attempted to burn down the Midshires bank in Hockley?" DS Dylan asked, a new formality in his voice.

Benson looked up. He shook his head from side to side.

"Who are you?" he asked.

Emma's flat was a short walk from Clarendon College, where she was retaking her A-levels. She'd got ten GCSEs, eight of them grade As. She found exams easy. But last year, when she was at the High School, she'd stopped trying. If her parents weren't going to try to save their marriage, why should she get good grades for them to boast about to their friends? She hated the sham that Dad put on for his constituents: *the family man with a loving wife and daughter, but isn't it a shame that they couldn't have more children?* Rubbish.

So, last year, she failed her exams deliberately. And she would fail them again this year, if she didn't start working soon. Emma's books lay open in front of her, but every time she looked at one, her eyes glazed over. It wasn't easy, being a famous politician's daughter. Even at the High School, she got funny looks sometimes. Teachers expected you to have opinions about things. Several kids crowed when Dad lost office. Until she got her own flat, boyfriends baulked at visiting Emma's home, in case they had to meet the father.

But Emma hadn't had any boyfriends recently. Her old High School friends were off at university, another world away. At college, Emma dressed down. No one there knew who her father was. No one really knew who she was: another anonymous student in a Mapperley Park bedsit. None of them cared if she lived or died.

The only people who really cared were her alcoholic mother and her philandering father. A few minutes ago, Dad phoned to see if she was in. Now he was coming over. Emma had never allowed him in the flat before. She didn't want the neighbours knowing who her father was. At this moment, she could hear his footsteps coming up the path. Even the way he rang the doorbell was characteristic, a ring and a half – insistent without being overbearing. He was a man who always got what he wanted.

But not this time.

Maggie Hansford was one of the four people who'd got a look at Phoenix during the Midshires bank attack. She'd been taken to hospital with shock and minor burns, and had been unable to describe anything about the arsonist, not even his anorak. Now, though, she had no doubts.

"That's him," she said, pointing to the middle of the identity parade. "Number four."

"You're sure?" Greasby prompted gently.

"Yes. I didn't think I'd recognize the bloke. But it was him. Definitely."

A few minutes later, they released Scott James and arrested Adam Benson.

Back in the CID offices, DI Greasby cracked open a bottle of Jameson's.

"A result," he said, "just when we thought we'd blown it. This is a definite cause for celebration."

The Phoenix team raised their glasses.

"What's your mate's name again?" Greasby asked Neil.

"Ben Shipman."

"To Ben Shipman."

They all drank.

"I spoke to Ian Jagger," Dad said, sitting awkwardly on the edge of Emma's one armchair. "Do you know who he is?"

Emma had seen the name. Some bigwig lawyer.

"Your girlfriend's boss?" she suggested.

From the look on Dad's face, Emma saw that she'd scored a hole in one. By "your girlfriend", Emma meant the black woman who she'd seen on Easter Monday, the night Emma told her father the big secret. Dad said then that the woman was a lawyer.

"Tell me," Dad said now, his voice dry and cracking. "Do you have any *proof* of what you told me the other night?"

"Do you think I'm stupid?" Emma asked. "All I have is the rubber stamp. And that's hidden. Wouldn't you like to know where?"

"You could easily have bought the rubber stamp after seeing the story in the papers."

"I could have," Emma said, "but I didn't."

"You see," Dad said, "Ian agreed with me. He said that you were almost certainly making the story up, like you made up the story about being pregnant, last year."

Emma laughed awkwardly, embarrassed to be reminded about that fiasco.

"But you don't think that, do you?" she sneered at her father. "You smelt the smoke on me that night. You *know* I'm telling the truth."

Dad gave a sad smile.

"No, Emma. I smelt nothing. In fact, Ian told me that he had a very good idea who the real arsonist was – a client of his – and he's arranged for the police to get this information."

"No," Emma said. "No, no, no."

"Yes," her father told her. "And if you listen to the radio news later today, you'll find out that the police have arrested a man in connection with the fires – Phoenix has been captured, Emma. It's over."

Emma stood up.

"Get out!" she yelled at her father. "Go on, get out!"

"I want to help, Emma," Dad told her, as he shuffled towards the door. "I want to…"

"You only ever want to help yourself," Emma said, slamming the door in his face. He thought it was all over. He had another think coming.

Still one and a half hours of tape to go. The camera panned the busy store. Neil watched as Clare scanned the Saturday shoppers, looking for one with more than a birthday present on his mind.

"Why are you still watching this?" he asked Clare, impatiently. "We've found Phoenix."

"But he's not confessed yet, has he?" Neil's girl-friend protested.

"Not to all of the attacks," Neil admitted. "But he's held up his hands to the Midshires bank. It's only a matter of time before he confesses to the rest."

"Still," Clare said. "If you had him on video, buying the stamp, it would help, wouldn't it?"

"Maybe," Neil conceded.

He didn't want Clare sitting there, watching grainy black and white videos. He was in a cele-bratory mood, and there was something he wanted to ask her. But he couldn't, not while she was glued to the screen. Then, to make things worse, Sam came in.

"Have you seen Steve? He was supposed to be cooking for me tonight."

That got Clare's attention.

"Ah." She ejected the tape from the machine and turned, uncomfortably, to Sam.

"I'm afraid I've got some bad news about Steve. I don't know how to put this." Clare hesitated. Sam didn't wait for Clare to explain. She groaned.

"You found out it was him, didn't you? The robberies."

Clare was incredulous.

"You *knew*?"

Sam shook her head.

"Not until the weekend. I worked it out. He lied to the police when I was out of the room. Ruth mentioned it to me in passing on Saturday. Evidently, Steve said he couldn't hear me while the Patels were being burgled because he had loud music on. He wasn't playing music. I'd have heard. Then I remembered about the loft – you know about the loft?"

Clare nodded. Sam went on.

"My ex-husband. He'd mentioned how there wasn't a proper wall separating the roof space. I confronted Steve and he admitted it. I told him he had to give Hilda's things back. She wasn't insured, you see. Then I told him I wanted the rest of the stuff out of the house."

"That was what he started doing last night," Clare told Sam, "but Ruth heard him."

"He'd already sold a couple of things to mates,"

Sam went on. "He planned to take the rest down the pub to sell there. I said he was a fool. He'd get caught. He ought to just dump it. I said if it wasn't gone today, I'd tell you."

She paused.

"Have I committed a crime?" Sam asked them. "By not telling you?"

"Technically," Clare said, as though there was a difference between a technical crime and a real one. "But we're off duty. I'd probably have done the same in your place."

Sam slumped in an armchair. Neil and Clare exchanged embarrassed glances.

"Look," Clare said, "I can see how awkward this is for you. Ruth and I will move out. Just give us a bit of time."

"Don't do that," Sam pleaded, sounding sincere. "I feel safer with you two around. No, it's Steve who has to leave … and quickly, before the neighbours find out it was him who burgled them. I'd have thrown him out sooner, only, he and I … we had a thing."

"I kind of guessed," Clare said.

"It was only for a few weeks," Sam said. "I was lonely and … he's just a big kid, you know? You can see what he's like. Always showing off. At first, I thought he was dead charming, so good looking…"

Clare avoided Neil's eyes. They heard a key turning in the lock.

"That'll be him," Clare said.

"Leave it to me," Sam told them. "I'll go and speak to him."

She left the room. For a moment, Neil worried that Clare was going to start the video again.

"You can't stay here after what's happened," Neil said. "Can you?"

"I don't see why not," Clare told him. "But I want to get out of the house now. Why don't we order a take-out from the Saagar and go back to your house to eat it?"

Neil smiled. The evening was starting to turn right after all.

"Let's do that," he said.

22

Jagger's offices were on the edge of the Park on Oxford Street, just round the corner from Nottingham Playhouse. The firm was housed in a large Victorian building which had been recently cleaned. The stone resembled speckled sand and it stood out from the similar buildings nearby.

Jagger's had better security than any building Emma had ever sneaked into. She'd already been in once, for a quick recce, but the receptionist immediately asked what she wanted. It was lunch hour, so Emma made up a story about being from a sandwich delivery service. Curtly, the receptionist informed her that she was in the wrong building. Emma couldn't risk going in and being seen a second time.

Emma considered coming back when the offices

were closed. She could pour petrol through the letterbox. But it was too chancy and too amateur. Emma had to find a way to get petrol inside and start the fire in the heart of the building, where flames wouldn't be spotted until the fire had had time to take hold. But she couldn't break in. She had no idea how to foil the burglar alarm. Also, from her quick glance around inside, it looked like the alarm worked on a sensor system. Therefore, even if she managed to sneak inside and hide until the office was closed, as soon as she started moving around, the alarm would go off.

There had to be another way. Emma got back into her car. On the passenger seat beside her was that day's *Evening Post* with its infuriating headline: "*PHOENIX ARRESTED!*" Emma hid her face behind the paper. She'd managed to find a two-hour parking space from which she could observe the solicitor's offices. She would wait and see.

Charlene drank her third mug of filter coffee since breakfast, but it did no good. She couldn't concentrate on the child custody appeal she was preparing. The work was detailed, and needed doing urgently. It was now Thursday afternoon, and the case was being heard on Friday morning. But it was hopeless. Yesterday evening, Ben had called to ask Charlene to come over after work today. He wanted to talk. Charlene already suspected what he was going to say. She'd been awake most of the night thinking about it.

How could he? How could he dump her after five years? And how could he do it straight after she'd given him the name of the serial arsonist? No: she had almost persuaded herself. He wasn't going to finish with her. There had to be another reason. But Charlene couldn't concentrate on work until she saw her boyfriend. She would go to him now and come back to the office afterwards.

"Just popping out," she told the receptionist, without explaining why. She shot out of the building. A familiar-looking girl in a beat-up old Renault 4 gave Charlene a funny look, then hid her face behind a newspaper. Charlene walked briskly to the multistorey car park next to the old General Hospital.

Charlene knew that she shouldn't be doing this. Work was meant to come first. But she would stay late to finish. Right now, she couldn't stop herself.

Clare got up at two. Sam was at work and Ruth was on duty. Steve seemed to be out, too, which was a relief. Clare couldn't believe that she'd been considering chucking Neil for a fling with Steve. He could have turned out even worse than Karl, who she went out with at university. Neil might be safe, rather than sexy, but he had a lot more things going for him than Steve ever would. Clare made herself toast and coffee, then plonked the Tableworks video into the machine. Today, she was going to get it out of the way, even though Neil was probably right: CID would get a confession before the day was over, and any video evidence would be unnecessary. Moreover, Adam Benson was the sort of person who had access to all sorts of stationery because of his job. He wouldn't need to buy a rubber stamp from Tableworks.

Clare started watching anyway. Funny, that Adam Benson turned out to be the arsonist. Clare had always half suspected that the arsonist was a woman, precisely because of the stamp. It was an oddly feminine touch, she thought, the stamp. And, traditionally, birds represented women, didn't they? Adam Benson, though, had a public school education. He would probably have picked up all that ancient mythology stuff there. And he had already confessed to one of the arsons.

Clare was so wrapped up in her thoughts that she almost missed the dark figure, bent over the rubber stamps. Most people who looked in the tray spent only a moment or two. This one, however, seemed to be looking for something specific. But that wasn't what caught Clare's attention most strongly. It was the ski hat which the person was wearing. There was something very familiar about that woolly hat. She had seen it the day after this was filmed, leaving the library.

Then the person walked away, without buying anything. Clare was annoyed. She'd been so sure. To be on the safe side, she rewound the tape, and watched it in slow motion. This time, she caught a glimpse of the person entering the shop: woolly hat, half trench coat. At first glance, it looked like a man, though it wasn't Adam Benson. Clare took another look, with freeze frame, at the thin, pale face. A bit of hair poked out from beneath the hat. The shape of the body was ambiguous. Even so, Clare was convinced. It wasn't a man. It was a girl.

But the person hadn't bought a stamp. Clare rewound again. Maybe the camera had missed it. There she was, looking through the tray. The camera moved on to cover the rest of the shop. Then, when it came back to the person in the dark trench coat, she was leaving. Clare looked at her hands as she stood up. Yes, they *were* a woman's hands. You could tell that, even though they were clenched. *Clenched*. Of course. With mounting excitement, Clare watched as Phoenix put her hand into her trench coat pocket, stealing the rubber stamp which would become her signature.

Then she rang Neil.

Ben was sitting in his small kitchen, reading the *Guardian*, when the doorbell rang. At least he was dressed. Some days, at this time, he was still in his dressing-gown. He went down the stairs. They were a funny collection, the people who called round when you were at home during the day, all of them trying to sell you something you didn't want. Ben opened the door, ready to respond with a polite "no thanks". Then he saw Charlene. She looked tired and vulnerable.

"I know, you weren't expecting me yet."

"It's fine," Ben fibbed. "Come in."

He'd been expecting her at six, or thereabouts. He'd thought he'd have time to think about what to say. Then, with work starting at ten, he'd have a ready-made excuse to leave. Instead, she'd come early, and caught him off guard. Clever of her.

"Have you eaten?" he asked.

His breakfast things were still on the table.

"I'm not hungry."

"Got the afternoon off?"

"No," Charlene said. "I have to go back. I'm probably going to have to work very late. That's why I came round now."

They sat down in the living-room. Ben chose the armchair rather than sitting next to her on the sofa. So now they were facing each other, ready for a confrontation. Charlene crossed her legs uncomfortably.

"Well?" she said.

Ben was tongue-tied.

"You wanted to talk," she said, making it sound like a statement in a court of law.

How did you finish with someone? He'd never actually done it before, never had a serious girlfriend before Charlene. Even now, Ben wasn't one hundred per cent certain that he wanted to. He wasn't certain what he wanted. Both of them, maybe, but neither Ruth nor Charly would ever agree to that. All he could do now was to tell the truth. So he blurted it out.

"I'm in love with someone else."

Charlene stared at him as though she didn't understand.

"Ruth?" she asked, incredulously.

"Yes."

"How … could…" She didn't finish the question because there were tears rolling down her cheeks. She pulled out a hanky. Ben leant forward to comfort her.

"No," she snapped. "Get away!"

Ben sat opposite Charlene, shivering, waiting for her to recover herself. When she did, her eyes were hard and cynical.

"You don't have the right to touch me any more," she said. "Understand?" Ben nodded. Her voice quivered.

"How did this happen?"

She made it sound like his relationship with Ruth was so strange that she needed scientific proof of its existence.

"You knew I was seeing her," Ben mumbled.

"Before…"

"I didn't stop," Ben confessed.

Charlene stared at Ben as though she was seeing him for the first time.

"She made you choose, didn't she?"

"Yes. She did."

Charlene began to stroke her forehead, the way she did when she had a headache.

"I … I don't understand what she's got. I've seen her. She's nothing. I mean … she's white … she's plain … she didn't go to university. What have you got in common with her?"

Ben wasn't going to let her insult Ruth like that.

"It's not your business, Charly."

"Don't call me Charly," she snapped. "I hate it when you call me Charly. I'm not a teenager any more, though maybe your new girlfriend is."

"The question," Ben said, slowly, "is what you and I have in common any more. You've changed, Charl … Charlene. You're not the person I fell in love with. You're harder, more … materialistic, less caring."

Charlene leant forward, so that she was almost shouting in his ear.

"Changed? Of course I've changed. You have to change to get by in the world, Ben. I'm learning to live in the real world, whereas you … you've changed too. You've turned into some kind of Uncle Tom imitation of Dixon of Dock Green and you want a homely white girlfriend to complete the image. You know what that is? It's sad."

Angrily, Charlene stood up to go, but she hadn't finished.

"You want to know what we've got in common? I'll tell you: our culture, our experience of being black in this country. Most of all, our history together. You're throwing those five years in my face, as though they weren't real. But they *were* real. What's happening now is unreal. It's stupid and sick." Her voice became softer, almost unbearably poignant.

"You want to know something even sicker? If you ever come to your senses, I'll take you back."

Ben didn't know what to say. He had never seen her more angry, more upset, or more beautiful.

"Because," she said in a softer voice, tears falling down her cheeks, "I love you. There's never been anyone other than you. Do you understand? No one. This is it for me. What we had happens once in a lifetime, and even then only if you're very lucky."

She opened the door. He could hardly hear her voice for the sound of crying, hers and his.

"I can't believe you're throwing it away," she said.

The receptionist left at five-thirty, but there were still people working inside. Immediately, Emma hurried to the door to let herself in. It was locked. She was on her way back to the car when a woman swept past her, a tall, elegant black woman who was sickeningly familiar: her father's girlfriend, Charlene. Emma had watched her leave two hours before. Emma followed Charlene to the steps of Jagger's, keeping her head down. But there was little chance of Charlene recognizing her. She seemed preoccupied. Indeed, she looked like she'd been crying.

Finding the door locked, Charlene reached into her handbag and got out some keys. She let herself in and, as she went through the door, Emma hurried after her. She caught the door to the solicitor's office just before it hit the latch. Then Emma waited for as long as she dared, giving Charlene time to get out of view before she pushed the door open.

The reception area was empty. Emma was safe, if she moved quickly. She darted across the hallway, hoping that no one heard the rattle of bottles in her brown briefcase. Footsteps were receding up the stairs. Emma took a chance and followed them. It would help if she was able to hear what was going on.

Charlene had gone into an office on the second floor. Emma heard the door close. There was a red bucket in the corridor. A cleaner was doing the rounds. Emma pressed her body to the wall at the top of the stairs, hoping not to be seen. Then she chanced another look. There was an office opposite

Charlene's with its door open. No noise came from it. Emma crouched down, then hurried to the office door.

The room was empty. A glance at the bin told Emma that the room had already been cleaned. She pushed the door to, so that it wasn't quite closed. Then, just in case, she crouched down in a space between the desk and the wall, much as she had squeezed into the small space at the library what seemed a lifetime ago. Emma put the briefcase down behind her. Then she waited.

"You could be right," Neil told Clare, "but it doesn't prove anything."

"Benson has only confessed to one attack," Clare argued, "not to being Phoenix. All right. So he did that one. It was a completely different MO to the others. But I reckon that the person on this video did the other four or five."

"Prove it," Neil said.

"Find the person on this video, and I will."

"Clare," Neil said, with what he thought was commendable self-restraint, "there isn't enough evidence on that video to convict the girl of shoplifting, never mind arson. But I'll tell you what. I'll take it in tomorrow, show it to Chris Dylan."

"He's already convinced that Benson's the arsonist."

"Not completely convinced," Neil told her.

"There's not enough to make it stand up in court, not unless Benson confesses. Believe me. I'll do what I can."

"Thanks," Clare said. "I'm sorry to keep harping on about this, but I spent all that time watching those tapes, and then…"

"I know," Neil said, "but let's talk about something nicer. How would you like to come round to mine on Saturday night? I'll cook you a nice candle-light supper. We can have a few drinks, a video, music…"

"Wine, women and song," Clare teased. "I'd love to." She looked at her watch. "Talking of food, I'd better go and buy something soon. I need a decent meal before going on night shift. Want to join me?"

"Better not," Neil said. "I promised I'd go round to my mum's."

"Give her my love."

Clare hugged Neil, then gave him a long, lingering kiss before she let go. He could hardly wait for Saturday.

"Still working?"

Charlene looked up. It was her boss.

"I have to get this finished for the morning."

"Earlier this week you had too little work. Now have you got too much?"

Charlene shook her head.

"I had something personal to sort out at lunchtime. It took longer than I thought. That's why my timing's out."

Jagger gave her a caring, but inquisitive smile.

"You and your policeman friend?"

Charlene nodded.

"It's over."

"I'm sorry to hear that."

Keep yourself together, Charlene kept telling herself. *You can't afford to break down in front of the boss again.*

"Yeah," she said, her chin quivering. "Me too."

"Listen," Ian said, softly. "Why don't you leave that? Come in early tomorrow, sort it out when your mind's fresh. Let me take you for a drink or a meal. You can get it all off your chest."

"Thanks," Charlene said. "I appreciate your being so caring, but ... I'm in court in the morning. I won't sleep well if I'm not prepared."

She laughed unconvincingly.

"I probably won't sleep anyway, but ... what the hell."

"I hope you won't leave us," Ian said, "now that your main reason for being in Nottingham has gone."

"No," Charlene promised. "I won't leave you."

Jagger got to the door.

"Oh," he said. "If you're to be the last out, you'll need the alarm code. Do you know it?"

"No."

"It's 1966. Memorize that, would you? Don't write it down."

"Easy. The year England won the World Cup."

When Jagger was gone, Charlene had another cry. The work would take her ages, because she couldn't concentrate. What time was it? The room was starting to get dark. Instead of turning the lights on, Charlene let her head drop to her desk. She had hardly slept the night before, worrying about Ben. Now that the worst had happened, maybe she could doze. If she could snatch a few seconds sleep, her mind would clear a little. She could crack through what work remained.

As Charlene's mind blurred, she thought she heard a noise, but it probably came from outside. She eased her mind into sleep by repeating the burglar alarm code, like a mantra: *1966, 1966, 1966, 1966...*

23

"So that's my theory about the serial arsonist," Clare told Ben. "It's a girl in her late teens, and she's laughing at us, because she thinks she's got away with it. Hey, are you listening?"

"Uh … sorry?"

Clare slowed the patrol car down.

"No wonder you let me drive tonight. You're miles away. What's on your mind?"

"I split up with Charlene today."

"Ah."

Clare drove in silence. This first half hour of the shift was usually quiet. Later, things would hot up. When Ben didn't speak for two minutes, she gave way to curiosity.

"Have you told Ruth yet?"

"When did I get a chance? She finishes work the same time I start."

"She should be getting home any time around now," Clare said. "I could stop by a phonebox..."

"I think I'd rather tell her in person," Ben said.

They stopped talking. The radio was quiet, too. None of the messages concerned them. They were a litany of fights in pubs, minor domestics and car break-ins: the casual cruelties of a normal Nottingham night. Until, suddenly, one came on which wasn't.

"Reports coming in of a fire at Wellington Circus," said the voice on the radio. "One report says that the Playhouse is on fire."

"Let's get over there," Clare said, as she began to accelerate. "This sounds like Phoenix."

The Playhouse was just outside their patch, but it was only a stone's throw from where they were patrolling.

"Will there still be a performance on?" Ben asked.

"They're usually over by ten," Clare told him, "which figures. Phoenix never hits occupied buildings."

"What about the bank?"

"The bank wasn't her."

A new report came over the radio.

"The fire reported is just off Wellington Circus on Oxford Street. It is not – repeat, *not* – the Play-house, but the offices of a solicitors, Jagger's. The

Fire Brigade are two minutes away."

Clare and Ben were even nearer. They skidded round the big roundabout at the top of Maid Marian Way, siren blaring.

"Jagger's?" Clare said. "Isn't that where…?"

"Yes," Ben told her. "It is."

Charlene's head was heavy. She wanted to stay asleep. But her neck was stiff, and there was an awful lot of noise outside. Shouting. Sirens. The lights were out. She switched on the lamp above her desk and saw smoke. Shit. The place was on fire. No wonder she had slept so heavily. That was what smoke did to you. It knocked you out, then the carbon monoxide in it killed you. That was how most fire victims died, she knew: not from burns, but from suffocating by smoke.

Charlene got up and staggered to the door. Flames were curling up the stairwell. She couldn't go down two floors that way. The fire escape was across the corridor. If she could make her way over there, she could get down safely. But the heat was too immense. And she was so tired…

Charlene pushed her way back into the room she'd just left, her head beginning to whirl.

Flames engulfed the lower part of the building. Ben didn't like to admit it to anyone, but seeing Jagger's offices in flames gave him a certain crude satisfaction. However, he had to wipe the smile off his face as the lawyer himself appeared. As the second fire engine arrived, Jagger pulled up in his vintage car and jumped out, an unlikely figure in jeans and a polo neck sweater. The lawyer came straight over to Ben.

"I hope you've got a fire-proof safe for your most valuable papers, sir."

"Of course I have," Jagger snapped. "I'm not worried about that. It's Charlene Harris. She might be in there."

Despite the heat, Ben felt the back of his neck turn cold.

"It's twenty to eleven. Surely…"

"She had a lot to do. Moreover, she was very tired, and upset, for reasons you know more about than I do. She was still there when I left at seven. I rang her flat. There's no one home."

Ben blasphemed.

"Which is her office?"

"That one."

There was a faint light coming from the room. His head pounding, Ben ran to the Watch Officer and yelled.

"I think there's someone on the second floor. She may be overcome by smoke."

"Which room?"

Ben pointed it out.

"We can't go in," the leading firefighter told him.

"It's not safe. We'll have to get the hydraulic high-rise in place."

"How long will that take?"

"Five minutes. Let's hope we've got that long. Wait."

The leading firefighter from the second engine pointed at the window.

"There she is. We'd better get a ladder."

Ben's heart sank. He hadn't really believed that Charlene was in there. But now he could see her, trembling at the window, trying to push it open. She must be nearly overcome by smoke. And yet, she had so much courage, Ben knew. She backed away from the window. He hoped she hadn't collapsed. If only...

A chair smashed through the window. Glass hurtled on to the ground below, some of it scratching Ben. He watched as the firefighters left their hoses. The room was ablaze. There wasn't even time for a ladder. Two of them were getting a canvas safety ring from one of their trucks, running forward, holding it like a trampoline. The Watch Officer called out.

"Give us a hand here."

Clare, Ben and Jagger rushed to help hold the large white circle. The Assistant Divisional Officer had arrived in his car. He produced a megaphone, and called up to Charlene, reassuring her that she would be safe. As Ben stared upwards, he told her to get ready.

"I'm going to count down for you to jump, from five to zero. Do you understand?"

Through the heavy screen of smoke, they could make out Charlene nodding.

"Five."

She kicked a bit of glass out of the window and stepped forward.

"Four."

She tried to get a balance on the edge of the window, but found it difficult because of the broken glass.

"Three."

For a moment, Ben thought that she was going to totter over, missing the safety ring completely.

"Two."

She seemed to tense her body, ready for the jump. Smoke was still billowing out of the window, but so were flames. Charlene's clothes were starting to catch fire.

"One."

Without waiting for zero, Charlene jumped. The world became slow motion. Ben watched her body glide, dividing the air like the tall, elegant bird she had always been, emerging from the smoke and flames into the night sky with one brilliant bound. She was, for a moment, a miraculous creature who had suddenly remembered how to fly.

Then her body began to fall.

They caught her.

24

Neil had just fallen asleep when the phone rang. The voice on the other end of the line was Clare's.

"What's wrong?" he asked, anxiously. "Are you all right?"

"Nothing's wrong with me," she told him. "But there's been another fire. Chris Dylan will be round at your house in five minutes to pick up that video."

"Can't it wait until morning?" Neil complained.

"They've got someone coming into the office with a digital scanner. They want the picture in the media by the morning."

"I'm getting up," Neil said. "Where was the fire?"

"At Jagger's," Clare told him. "Charlene was inside at the time. Now I've got to go."

She hung up the phone. Neil spoke to the silent receiver.

"I'm coming in," he said.

From a safe distance, Emma watched the conflagration. She was relieved that the Fire Brigade had saved Charlene. Emma would never have started the fire if she'd known that the lawyer was still inside. The place had been quiet for so long that Emma assumed Charlene had left and forgotten to put the alarm on. It was kind of poetic justice, though, catching her father's girlfriend in the fire … even if Dad protested that Charlene *wasn't* his girlfriend.

Emma wondered if her father knew what had happened. When the last fire engine had gone, and she was sure that no one was looking, Emma started the car, then drove on to Derby Road and into the Park. Despite the hour, there was still a light on in her dad's living-room. Good. But then Emma noticed another car parked outside, a vintage one. Dad's solicitor had got there before her.

Emma didn't mind waiting. She had no intention of talking to her dad's solicitor, but nor was she tired. The energy buzz from the fire would keep her up all night. She turned the engine off and remembered the last time she'd been round to Dad's flat, a few short days ago. Then, she'd interrupted his squalid little seduction.

"Emma, what are you doing here?" Dad had said, looking embarrassed as hell.

"I had a row with Mum," she'd lied, not wanting Charlene to know what she was going to tell Dad, that she'd just burnt down a petrol station.

"But I thought you weren't staying with your mother any more?"

"It's a long story."

"Excuse me," Charlene had said.

She got up awkwardly because there was a broken strap on her dress and she was holding it in place. Charlene hurried past Emma into the hall.

"Who's she?" Emma asked, not trying to disguise the contempt in her voice. "Another of your secretaries?"

"She's a lawyer. A very good one."

"So that's why she's here at one in the morning with her dress half off?"

Her father put on his usual condescending voice.

"If you'll just give me a moment alone with her, Emma."

Emma didn't move. She looked around as her father blundered into the hallway where Charlene was putting on her coat. Emma's father whispered.

"Charlene. I'm sorry…"

"Save it. I'm going."

"Let me call you a taxi."

"I can walk. It's not far. Remember?"

Her father showed the woman to the door. Emma

gloated. Lawyer? She looked more like a model. At the door, Dad tried to give her a peck on the cheek, but Charlene swept out. She had more class than Emma's dad did.

Next, Dad came back into the dining-room.

"What the hell do you mean, bursting in on me like that?"

"You told me to treat the place as my home, remember?"

Dad sat down and took a large swig of his drink. There was a glass that Charlene had left behind. Emma picked it up and drank the brandy in two gulps.

"And what's all this about you arguing with your mother?" Dad said. "You haven't lived with your mother since Christmas."

"You couldn't have lived with her either," Emma told him. "Not the way she's been since you walked out on her. At least I go and see her every week. All she does is drink and cry all day."

"I support her and I support you. I even bought you a car for your eighteenth. What more do you want? Are you going to fail your A-levels again?"

"Probably," Emma said. "I only do it to punish you."

Dad yawned. She hated it when he yawned when you were talking to him.

"Don't try that one again, Emma. I've warned you before, if you don't get to university this year, I won't support you. I mean it."

"I don't give a damn."

Dad lit a cigar.

"Anyway, what was it you wanted? What was so important that you had to interrupt my evening?"

"I've been busy," Emma told him. "I wanted to tell you about it."

"What do you mean?"

"I've put on a little show for you. It'll be in the papers tomorrow. It's probably on the radio news now. But you can read about it tonight."

"Look, Emma, I haven't got the time for silly games."

"Don't call me Emma. That's not my name any more."

"What are you talking about?"

Emma smiled and produced a small wooden block from her pocket. She showed it to her father.

"Call me Phoenix."

That took him by surprise. Emma went on to tell him about the petrol station fire that night. Dad kept saying:

"Why? I don't understand why."

But it was a stupid question. He understood all right, and he knew that he could do nothing about it. He couldn't give Emma up to the police. She could imagine the headlines now.

"WELLY DRIVES WIFE TO DRINK AND DAUGHTER TO ARSON. 'PHOENIX' IS

DAUGHTER OF FORMER CABINET MINISTER."

No matter what he said, Dad probably dreamt of returning to power one day. With a story like that in the papers, he'd be lucky to hold on to his seat and his directorships.

Dad's next move was exactly what she'd expected. He started talking about therapy. That was when Emma left, knowing that Dad would have the constant worry of wondering whether the arson story would come out. It wouldn't, not unless he told someone. She'd been so careful.

But the stupid man hadn't trusted Emma not to get caught. He had told someone: Jagger, who was in the flat now. Emma didn't know much about the solicitor, but he was obviously a devious sod. He had set somebody else up for the series of arsons, giving him the credit. He deserved to have his offices burnt down.

Emma watched as Jagger finally left the flat, got into his car, and drove away. It was nearly three in the morning. She got out of her car, then, using the key Dad had given her, let herself into the apartment. Dad was on the stairs, going up to bed. He was hunched over a little and looked old. Emma's father turned round in time to see her smiling victoriously at him.

"Hi, Dad!" she said.

*　　*　　*

Ben sat by Charlene, waiting for her to recover consciousness. She'd been out for two hours now, and might sleep all night. Ben would stay there, whatever happened. Questions kept crossing his mind. Was it his fault? If he hadn't finished with her today, surely she wouldn't still have been at work. Should he call her parents? The doctors said that she was in no danger. Waking Mr and Mrs Harris in the middle of the night would give them a real scare. But suppose something went wrong? They'd want to be with her.

Ben decided to postpone ringing the Harrises until Charlene was conscious. They would take it much better if they were able to talk to their daughter, have Charly reassure them that she was fine. Yes, that was the right thing to do.

Charlene breathed steadily, making the occasional rasping noise. The doctors said that there was some smoke damage to her lungs, but it shouldn't prove lasting. Thankfully, she hadn't sustained any burns. He couldn't bear to think of her beautiful body damaged in that way. It hurt him to realize how close she'd come to...

"Ben?"

A hoarse whisper. Her eyes blinked open.

"Charly?"

"What are you doing here?"

He smiled and took her hand.

"Where else would I be?"

"I don't … I don't…"

She looked confused for a moment. Her eyes lost focus and her head seemed to sink back into the pillow. Then she blinked awake and spoke again.

"Did you save my life?"

"No," Ben said. "You saved your own life."

Charly nodded.

"But you were there?"

"I'll always be there for you."

She gripped his hand tightly.

"I'll hold you to that."

There was a knock on the ward door. Ben turned to see a head poke around it. Neil.

"Is she awake?" he whispered.

"Barely."

"I've got the picture."

"Are you up to looking at a photograph?" Ben asked, gently.

"I guess."

Ben nodded at Neil. He came in, holding a computer print-out.

"We've enhanced it a bit," he said. "It's still not much of a likeness." He handed Charlene the picture.

"*I'm supposed to recognize somebody from this?*" Charlene said.

"I know it's not very good, but…"

"Wait," Charlene said. "There is something familiar about her."

She put the picture down and closed her eyes. Ben thought that she'd gone back to sleep. But then she spoke.

"The girl's called Emma Wellington," she said. "I don't know where she lives, but I can give you her father's address."

She told it to them. Then she let go of Ben's hand.

"Now get out of here, both of you," she ordered. "I need to sleep."

"I hate you," Emma told her father. "I hate everything you stand for. Do you understand that? You take people and you use them. Like that man who was done for being Phoenix. I'm Phoenix, not him."

"He started one of the fires," Dad said, in his patient but exasperated voice. "I didn't use him. All I did was protect you."

"I don't want your protection," Emma insisted. "You need mine. Because if I tell people who Phoenix really is, you'll be the one in trouble."

Dad shook his head slowly, then gazed at her like a judge about to pass sentence.

"You need help, Emma. I can't let you carry on this way. You nearly killed someone tonight."

"That was an accident."

"It doesn't matter whether you intended it. You're an adult, Emma. You recklessly endangered property and lives. The crime carries a life sentence."

Emma refused to take this in.

"Anyway," she went on, "I told you. Phoenix is finished. They'll never catch me. There's no evidence against me. Only a little wooden block with a rubber stamp on the end of it, and I can burn that."

"Can you?"

"Wouldn't you like to know where I've hidden it?"

"I can't let you get away with this, Emma. Ian Jagger says that if you give yourself up, see a psychiatrist, it may never come to trial."

"Give myself up? You've got to be kidding."

Her father stared at her with sunken, sympathetic eyes.

"You need help," he said.

Emma couldn't believe it.

"What are you saying, Dad? That you'd give up your own daughter? Even you wouldn't sink that low. Do you know what it would do to your career?"

Dad didn't stop staring at her. It was creepy.

"I'm past caring about my career," he said.

There was a dreadful four in the morning silence. Then the doorbell rang. Emma jumped to her feet.

"Who?"

"I don't know," Dad said. "I suppose I'd better answer it."

He went to the door. Emma heard the two men identifying themselves. One of them was Dylan, who she'd seen on TV. The other was younger.

Emma was tired, she realized suddenly, and her brain was slowing down. She ought to be trying to escape. Did this flat have a back entrance? She didn't know. It was too late anyhow. She would have to play it cool. They had no evidence. They couldn't have.

"Emma Wellington?" said the younger of the two detectives. "I'm arresting you under the Criminal Damage Act, 1971. You do not have to say anything, but it may harm your defence if you do not mention when questioned something which you later rely on in court. Anything you do say may be given in evidence. Do you understand?"

Emma nodded. As the young officer handcuffed her, Dad spoke.

"There's something here you need."

To Emma's utter astonishment and disgust, Dad walked over to the fireplace and took one of the trophies from above it, then handed it to Dylan. Emma knew very well which trophy it was – his Parliamentarian of the Year award from *The Spectator*. Dylan took off the lid and looked inside. He saw the rubber stamp.

"Have you touched this, sir?"

Dad shook his head.

"But you knew it was there?"

"Yes. You may want to take the electric typewriter from my study, too."

The young officer went for it. Dylan spoke again.

"I'm afraid I may have to charge you, sir, for covering this up."

"I understand," Dad said in a tired voice. "I'll explain."

Dad held out his hands for the cuffs. Emma suddenly felt sorry for him, and began to wonder what she had done.

"That won't be necessary, Mr Wellington."

DS Dylan led them out, allowing Dad time to set the burglar alarm before he locked the front door. As she sat beside her father in the back of the car, Emma's mind went blank. She was suddenly relieved that it was all over.

EPILOGUE

Neil had impressed himself with the meal: sea-food pie with a nice bottle of dry white wine, followed by Marks and Sparks' chocolate mousse. Now it was late. They'd talked about the Phoenix case, but it hadn't dominated the conversation. Clare had been proved right about the video, and she was a magnanimous victor. The girl who'd called herself Phoenix had already been bailed into psychiatric care.

"What will happen to Wellington?" Clare asked, as he poured the coffee. "How will this affect his political career?"

"No comebacks for him," Neil said. "He's addressing his constituency association tonight – some kind of an emergency meeting. They say he's going to offer to stand down at the next election, but they might demand that he resign straight away."

"Nice coffee," Clare said, putting down her mug. "I suppose whether Welly resigns depends on whether he gets prosecuted for not revealing that his daughter was behind the fires."

"He won't be prosecuted," Neil said. "All he has to say is that he didn't believe her when she told him. He only found the rubber stamp that night and it was then that he worked out she'd been using his typewriter, too."

"But if he didn't believe her," Clare protested, "how come his friend Jagger fed Charlene the files showing that Adam Benson was involved? Surely they were trying to create a smokescreen, to protect Emma?"

She was right, Neil knew. But it wouldn't stand up in court.

"Wellington would say it was coincidence," Neil said. "That's what Jagger will tell Charlene, too. After all, Benson really did do the attack on the bank."

"Do CID believe the coincidence?"

Neil shook his head.

"Has Ruth heard from Ben yet?" he asked, changing the subject.

"No," Clare said, sadly. "He's still spending all his time with Charlene. She was discharged from hospital this afternoon. I think she's going to stay with her parents while she convalesces."

They cuddled up on the comfortable, second-hand settee.

"That was a lovely meal," Clare said. "Thank you."

They kissed.

"Actually," Neil murmured, when they eventually broke apart, "there's something I've been meaning to ask you."

"Ask away," Clare said, her head flopping on to his shoulder. "Tonight, I'm in a mood to say 'yes' to almost anything."

"In that case," he said softly, stroking the back of her neck the way she liked, "let me ask you this."

He slid off the sofa, down on to his knees, and looked earnestly into her pale blue eyes.

"Clare Coppola, will you marry me?"

Look out for the next exciting instalment from

in
Asking For It

Some people invite you to burgle them. Some still leave doors and windows open. Others have locks which can be opened with a credit card in less time than it takes to pick a pocket. Failing that, some have doors which collapse with the first kick. They have ground floor windows which cannot be seen from the street. Their neighbours make so much noise, they wouldn't hear a bomb going off, unless it happened in their living room. Yes, some people are asking to be burgled.

The thief doesn't accept every invitation. Being lazy, he only goes for places where the pickings are easy, the risks minimal. Once, he went after the usual: videos, TVs, hi-fi. But these items are bulky and conspicuous, therefore dangerous. Nowadays, he prefers to take things which fit snugly into his shoulder bag: CDs, watches, cameras, calculators. Best of all: chequebooks, chequecards, credit cards. Ideally: cash.

Where to steal from? The richest pickings used to be from the prosperous middle classes. But now they've got burglar alarms and neighbourhood watch schemes. They're best left to the professionals, who can be in and out in a minute, taking a baseball bat to anyone who gets in their way.

The children of the middle classes, however, are a different story. They have all the consumer goods, but none of the security. They're so casual about their possessions, you'd think they want to be burgled. It gives them something to talk about with their friends, one more reason to complain about the world.

The thief wanders around a university hall of residence on a Friday afternoon in early May. This hall has been good to him before, so he's hopeful. His usual technique is to show up in the morning, slipping into rooms just after their occupants have gone off to lectures. It's easy to tell which rooms are empty because the pigeonholes in the foyer will be empty, too. Friday afternoons aren't so good. The place is nice and quiet. Plenty of people are out. Some of them have gone away for the weekend. Sadly, they've taken their wallets and purses with them. All the thief's picked up so far are a bunch of indie CDs, an Olympus AF10 and a CD Walkman with portable speakers.

The stuff in his bag will bring in forty, maybe fifty pounds. But the thief wants more. He wants enough money to have a really good weekend. So he climbs another set of stairs, walks stealthily down another corridor, looking for one more room with "burgle me" scrawled on its welcome mat. With each set of stairs, there's more risk – he has further to run if challenged. The first rule of burglary is this: have a safe escape route planned – and he has. Each floor has a fire door – not alarmed – which can be opened from the inside, but not out.

The room he's going to try next had nothing in its pigeon hole. The thief knocks on the door. No reply. There's a decent sized gap between the door and its side post. The thief pulls a Visa card from his jeans pocket, pushes it into the gap so that the spring bolt is pushed back. He presses the door, wiggles the credit card and – *hey presto!* – he's in.

The room is practically empty. There's a bunch of text books on the shelf, some notes on the desk. There's a poster saying *Jesus Saves* above it. The thief looks under the bed. He goes through the desk. He looks behind the books. Finally, he pulls out the Bible, holding it open with his gloved hands so that any enclosures flutter to the ground. Out falls a shiny, plastic credit card. A broad smile fills the thief's face.

The name on the card is male, which is useful.

The thief can learn to copy the signature, then use it himself, rather than selling it on for a pittance. The way it's hidden suggests that the credit card's owner has been keeping it for emergencies. He'll have been cautious about using it, even though the credit limit will only be five or six hundred pounds. The thief will be cautious, too. He intends to get full value out of this card.

The thief tidies up quickly. If he leaves the room as he finds it, then, hopefully, it will be a few days before the victim notices that the card's gone. Maybe he won't find out until he suddenly gets a huge bill.

Satisfied that the room is straight, the thief checks that the corridor is clear, then slips out. He intends to leave the building, dump his takings in a safe place, then shoot into town for a spending spree on the credit card.

The thief reckons without the guy who charges out of his room on the floor below, barging into the thief as he passes, knocking the bag from his shoulder to the floor. The guy trots down the stairs without an apology. The thief watches the guy go, clocking his ugly, arrogant face. The guy doesn't look back at the thief, which is good. Then the thief looks back at the door through which the guy has just come. It's ajar.

If ever a guy was asking for it, it's this one. The thief picks up his bag and nudges the door open. He can still feel the throb in his shoulder from where the guy knocked against him. He will enjoy...

Something's wrong. A single glance tells the thief that this isn't a guy's room, it's a girl's room. In fact, the thief remembers, all the rooms on this floor are for women. And this one's a mess. There are clothes, cassettes, books and stuff scattered across the floor. The bed is made, yet there's the unmistakeable smell of sex. The thief realizes that he's made a mistake, that he ought to leave the room quickly, before...

Then he hears a whimpering sound, coming from the side of the bed. Common sense tells him to get out of the room this moment. A smaller, but more insistent voice tells him to stay.

"Are you all right?" he calls, softly, before taking a step forward, looking.

On the floor, a naked girl with short hair pulls a towel around her bruised body.

"Help me," she says.

Other books by David Belbin in

P●INT CRiME

AVENGING ANGEL

Traffic's murder tonight…

Clare and Neil of The Beat meet as they
investigate Clare's brother's death…

BREAK POINT

Game, set and … murder…

FINAL CUT

Lights, camera … murder…

SHOOT THE TEACHER

Even teachers don't deserve to die…

DEADLY INHERITANCE

Blood is thicker than water…